ℒOVE ℬITES

A SUGAR CITY NOVELLA

Falling in love is like swimming with sharks…

Sharona Blaire is only in Australia for a business audit, but she's determined to make the most of her one free night. So when she spills her drink on a handsome stranger and they end up flirting, she does something completely out of character—she kisses him. But the prospect of taking it further totally freaks her out…almost as much as discovering the next morning that the man she's auditing is the sexy, tanned stranger she left with zero explanation.

An audit during his crew's most important expedition yet is a complication marine biologist Jeff Cruz doesn't need—especially when the auditor is the gorgeous, fascinating woman from the night before. Out at sea with nowhere to run, he's forced to admit Sharona draws him in like a shark to blood. But Jeff's one passion is his job, and nothing—not even love—will get its hooks in him…

LOVE BITES

A SUGAR CITY NOVELLA

OPHELIA LONDON

Entangled Publishing, LLC
2614 South Timberline Road
Suite 109
Fort Collins, CO 80525
Visit our website at www.entangledpublishing.com.

Bliss is an imprint of Entangled Publishing, LLC. For more information on our titles, visit http://www.entangledpublishing.com/category/bliss

Edited by Alycia Tornetta
Cover design by Jessica Cantor

Ebook ISBN 978-1-63375-047-0
Print ISBN 978-1-50084-324-3

Manufactured in the United States of America

First Edition August 2014

Dedicated to Peter Benchley, Steven Spielberg and Roy Scheider for being first to hook my imagination and irrational fear/fascination with great white sharks.

Chapter One

If the universe was keeping score, it would be Universe: 2 Sharona Blaire: 0

This is so *not my day.*

Though technically, today had begun thirty-six hours ago.

Her current condition could be blamed on turbulence and the guy in the seat next to her who'd been making nonstop jokes since he'd boarded in Brisbane about this being Sharona's first trip to "the bush."

Aussie humor.

While gripping a Bloody Mary in one hand, she just needed to stretch her legs after the million-hour flight from Miami. She hadn't meant to wander into first class; it was the siren call—or rather scent—of warm chocolate chip cookies that drew her that way.

No one got cookies in coach.

After receiving the stink eye from a hovering flight

attendant, Sharona was just about to return to her seat when a jolt of turbulence rocked the plane and the scary FASTEN SEAT BELTS light illuminated. So, obviously she hadn't *meant* to spill her tomato juice concoction on the guy wearing a sleep mask in 3A.

Most of it landed on her, anyway…

"I'm so sorry," Sharona panic-whispered as stink-eye flight attendant took her by the elbow and ushered her up the aisle, back to her seat. She was pretty sure the man heard her rushed apology because there were definite vocal clues that he was now wide awake. Once she was strapped in, the flight attendant tossed Sharona a few napkin squares to lap up the Bloody Mary splattered all over her shirt like a crime scene. When it was obvious she was only making it worse, she sat back, closed her eyes, and tried very hard to ignore her seatmate the rest of the way to Sydney.

Maybe it was karma who saw fit that her suitcase was stuck in Brisbane, even though Sharona hadn't disembarked there. But karma was such a bitch. So, with her wheelie carry-on bag squeaking behind her, she was forced to stroll — as nonchalantly as possible — through Sydney International Airport, grab a cab, and check into her hotel room…all while looking like she'd just stabbed someone. Awesome.

Two hours later, Sharona curled one hand around the stem of her glass while the other tugged at her too-short hem. What had possessed her to purchase a little black dress instead of a practical outfit she would wear again after tonight, she still couldn't fathom.

She took in the dimly lit bar, the business meetings, vacationing couples, and other hotel guests. It wasn't late, but she felt herself craving a huge, slack-jawed yawn and to inconspicuously lay her head on the mahogany bar and pass out. According to her internal clock, it was the day after tomorrow.

Her travel arrangements had been so sudden that she hadn't figured out the time zone difference.

Let's see…if it was 10:00 a.m. when I left Miami, and we flew ahead fourteen hours, plus crossed over the International Date Line, and *the Bermuda Triangle…what is the exact Greenwich Mean Time?*

Wow. The math was way too exhausting. This might be her one and only free night in Sydney, however, and she refused to spend it crashed out in her hotel room with the blackout shades drawn.

Oh, but how lovely did those blinds sound? And she was pretty sure there might still be some tomato juice in her ear.

Instead of crawling back to her hotel room and crashing, she *should* have been preparing for tomorrow. She'd scanned the files Garry sent with her on the plane, but when she'd tried to do an additional internet search about the head of the research team she'd been sent to meet, her stomach had decided to do the airsick tap dance. The remainder of the nineteen-hour flight over the ocean had been spent gripping her seat while talking herself out of losing her lunch. And the Bloody Mary incident had done nothing to boost her mood.

A happy-looking couple beside her clinked wineglasses and started in on the "Cheers, darling," "Oh, cheers to *you*, darling," routine. Maybe hanging at a bar wasn't such a hot idea. Since breaking off her engagement six months ago, she'd spent the appropriate amount of time being bitter. Once that faded, she'd decided she could do very well without the whole relationship thing.

Yet here she was, sitting in a bar attempting to be social instead of working.

"Aw, screw it," she said aloud, already imagining the pleasure of unzipping her dress, kicking it to the floor, and crawling into bed "au naturel," seeing as how she still hadn't received her lost suitcase.

Just as she held up her glass, about to down the rest of her tall Long Island iced tea, her elbow bashed into something rock hard.

"Whoa, there. Careful."

Sharona jerked and swiveled around, in the process, spilling her drink down the front of the person behind her.

Not. Possible.

"Oh, gosh, damn—I'm sorry!" She grabbed a coaster napkin off the bar and dabbed at the spot on the white button-down shirt that was now soaking wet.

"No worries." The voice was deep, and as she slid her gaze up from the wet chest to the face, she caught a pair of piercing blue eyes.

Hello, gorgeous…

"Hi," she said, getting that silly, short of breath sensation.

"Hi there."

The bright eyes paired with a crooked smile knocked her even more breathless. His grin was an interesting cross between Han Solo and Thor. Wowzers. Straight white teeth flashed behind the smile, and a five-o'clock-shadowed jaw— sharp enough to slice deli meat—made the whole visual package about an inch above Hollywood perfection. Before she could hear "Love is a Many Splendored Thing," the guy glanced down at her hand, which was more or less stroking his damp chest with a mind of its own.

"Sorry." She pulled it back and dropped the napkin. "I can't believe I did that twice in one day."

"Twice?" he said, a single eyebrow arching, again with the Han Solo charisma. "We just met."

She shouldn't have been surprised at his thick Australian accent. She did love an accent. Even the twangy drawls from Texas—that made every man sound like Rhett Butler—made Sharona uncharacteristically swoony.

"I meant that's the second time today I spilled my drink on a stranger," she explained, tucking some of her long dark hair behind an ear, then pushing her mostly empty glass all the way to the back of the bar. It only held a few chunks of ice, but why give karma any ammo? "You're number two, but the first was on an unfortunate passenger on my flight. Tomato juice—tragically. And the glass was full to the rim."

It was easy to laugh off the embarrassing event now, since there was no one in the bar that would know about it.

The guy's big blue eyes held on her for a long moment, and then he chuckled and leaned against the bar. He had broader-than-average shoulders, and with the sleeves of his shirt rolled up, she caught a pair of very impressive, suntanned arms. Her eyes were having a hard time deciding which place to focus.

Arms…eyes…shoulders…eyes…arms…eyes…mouth… oh, mouth…

"So…" He cut into her thoughts. "That was you, eh?"

Sharona blinked. "What?"

He brushed at his collar like he was dusting off lint. "At first I thought I was dreaming, because why would it be raining on an airplane? Unless the tropical weather followed

us from Miami."

As his words slowly processed, it felt like the floor was sliding out from under her. And she had nothing to grab onto but his arm. "You're not serious." She held on tight, without thinking. "*You're* who I…on the…?"

He nodded. "And it wasn't just tomato juice. I definitely tasted vodka."

"No…" Heat of mortification began creeping up her neck, no doubt accompanied by the *attractive* blotchy, red flush she'd worn like a banner since her awkward adolescence stage. "I can't believe I…"

He chuckled, then patted her hand that was still death-gripping his arm. A second later, she had the good sense to remove it.

"I heard you apologize," he said, "but by the time I got off my mask, you were gone."

"I'm so sorry. Please let me pay your dry-cleaning bill or…whatever you want me to do—just name it and I'll do it, I'll… No, I mean…" She paused to blow her hair back from her face; now even her ears felt hot. "Okay, this is officially the most humiliating day of my life."

His crooked smile turned into a laugh, a deep, manly sound. Its vibration registered at the back of Sharona's neck by way of delicate pinpricks, reminding her that she hadn't felt those kinds of pinpricks in a long time.

"You seem all right now. Not a drop of Bloody Mary." He eyed her dress, lingering on the low cut of the neckline.

"That's because the airline lost my bag and this outfit is brand new." She recrossed her legs, a bit more pleased with her wardrobe choice. "They swore it'd be delivered tonight. I grabbed this at the hotel gift shop, the shoes and everything, so I wouldn't mistakenly get arrested for murder. I should've bought jeans instead of"—she waved down at herself—"all this."

"I think you look...*very* nice." The way he said it, with a slight pause and that sexy accent, made Sharona forget all about jet lag. Instead, she was on high flirt alert.

"Thanks. I keep expecting to get a phone call any second that my bags are here. Actually..." She picked up her cell from the bar, reading the calendar event that had just popped up. She needed to remember to call Natalie.

"That the airline then?" His blue gaze darted to her phone.

"Reminder to call my best friend. It's her birthday tomorrow." She bit her lip. "Or today... I'm not sure of the time difference."

He laughed, sending another shock of pinpricks up her neck.

Hmm, if he keeps holding this kind of close eye contact with me, goodness knows what I'll do. Before her mind had the chance to wander too far, another of her teenage nervous habits took over, and thus commenced a burst of flirt-babble.

"No matter what time it is back home, I could probably call Natalie and she'd be awake. She's always awake when she's busy with work stuff—though I call it *obsessed*. She just started a new project and she's pretty passionate about it—obsessed, right? Or, you know, it could be all the sugar."

"Sugar?" Blue Eyes asked, shifting a few inches closer. The movement slowed her down, though her heart skipped a beat.

"Yes, she, um, she works at the Hershey factory and gets

to be around chocolate all day."

"Ahh, dream job." He gave her a knowing nod, the front of his wavy, dark hair falling across his forehead.

"For Natalie, pretty much. I talked to her a few days ago. She's having, um…emotional challenges with a new guy on her research team." She bent toward him like they were sharing a secret, twirling a strand of hair. "She had a major crush on him in high school, and now he's got her all"—she caught his eye—"hot and bothered, you know?"

In response, he cocked an eyebrow. "I do know. Though it's not a brilliant move to mix business and pleasure." He stared forward for a moment, then back at her as he ran a finger along the rim of his glass. "But I wonder how long I could resist if I were surrounded by something as tempting as chocolate."

"Agreed." Sharona laughed and set her phone on the bar, drumming her fingers on the face. "It's annoying though, not having my luggage. I've got an early job tomorrow and have to leave first thing. In and out, then back home. "

"You're only here for one night?" he asked, waving to the bartender, then pointing at Sharona's drink to refill. He was suave, this one.

She nodded slowly, wondering what she should read into his question.

"In and out, eh? Your career sounds interesting."

The one thing Sharona did not want to talk about was her job. "It's not really. What about you? Traveling on business"—she paused to shrug—"or pleasure?"

Well, that's not cliché at all.

She'd always been pretty crap at making flirty chitchat with strangers. But something about being halfway around the world made her feel…unencumbered. Or maybe it was the effects of her Long Island iced tea combined with his dreamy, ocean-blue eyes.

"I grew up not far from Sydney," he said. "But I'm also here just for the night." He lifted his glass and took a drink. Beer. Manly, no flare. She liked that. She also liked how he wasn't forthcoming with his personal info, either. It made the exchange more…mysterious—dangerous—yet it also felt safe to not know anything.

She'd been meaning to have an adventure, to bust out and get back to living, like Natalie had been begging her do to for the last few months. Hooking up with a tall, dark stranger in a bar wasn't anywhere on her to-do list, but as she eyed those broad shoulders, the thick neck, strong-looking hands, and gorgeous mouth…

What the hell, maybe he should be on the *top* of her "to-do" list.

She didn't have a ton of experience with the whole casual-sex thing. Okay, *zero* experience. But wasn't she due a little excitement after the sucky last few months? She glanced up at him through her lashes and when their eyes met, she giggled at the sexy place her mind had jumped.

"What?" he asked, tipping his head toward her. Man… he even smelled delicious.

"I was about to say something like, 'What a coincidence we're both here for one night,' but since it's a hotel, it's not coincidental in the slightest."

"Think of it this way," he rubbed a fist under his square jaw, "if we hadn't been on the same flight or at the same hotel, you would've had no one to spill your drinks on."

"Sorry, again," she said, touching his arm. *That rock of a bicep.* She could squeeze it all day.

When she purposefully didn't remove her hand after the socially acceptable amount of beats, he glanced at it for a moment, then his gaze drifted north to her lips.

Her mouth started to water as heat tiptoed up her spine, tingling at the nape of her neck. Was it the idea of kissing him—a total stranger—or was it the thought of doing something even semireckless after twenty-six years of playing it safe?

She could practically hear Natalie's voice in her head: *In the real world, people have one-night stands all the time. Go on, girl. Live a little!*

Why had Sharona always been so uptight about that sort of thing? Always needing a committed relationship—or at least the assurance that the commitment was on the horizon—before any fun, naked time. She'd been careful like that in her last relationship, and that had exploded in her face…an on-going explosion, actually.

Blue Eyes eased onto the bar stool at her side, and his knee pressed against her bare leg, at the same time, he reached for a napkin, brushing her hand. Whether the moves were intentional or not, another excited shiver sizzled at the back of her neck, heat unfolding inch by inch. Up close, he smelled even more amazing—and were those tiny freckles splashed across his nose?

She'd never thought this about a real-life man before, but…this guy was spectacular. Never had she experienced such intense, instant chemistry, not even with the man she almost freakin' married.

"So," Blue Eyes said, just before Sharona could get angry about Garry all over again, "you're passing through

Sydney but you won't tell me why." He leaned one of his toned arms on the bar. "You know that makes you irresistibly mysterious."

Sharona opened her mouth, ready to launch in about her assignment and the stress and terror and baggage that went along with it. But then she wondered if it might be more interesting to play the cryptic card for once. After all, it could be fun pretending to be something she wasn't for one night.

Whether the responsible side of her would have the guts to go through with anything past flirting was another story.

"Mysterious," she echoed, toying with the ends of her hair like she'd seen Natalie do. "You couldn't have described me better, Blue Eyes."

"You're making that up!"

Jeff couldn't help laughing as the woman at his side tossed her head and giggled, shoving him playfully on the shoulder. He hadn't meant to park himself next to the curvy brunette two hours ago, but oh, how revved he was now.

He shouldn't have been in the pub at all, but the thought of being at sea tomorrow made him drop in for a relaxing pint. When he'd gone to settle the bill, he'd had the little surprise of the woman in black spilling her drink all over him. Again. He hadn't exactly lied when he'd said her in-flight Bloody Mary had barely splashed him. He'd most likely have to throw that shirt away. Which he didn't mind—especially now. Talking to the beautiful American with the great legs and killer smile put him in a very…forgiving mood.

$\mathcal{L}$OVE $\mathcal{B}$ITES

"It's true," he said when they'd both stopped laughing. "My brothers and I were forced to take etiquette classes, every Saturday for two months. I told my mates I was visiting my grandmother, which seemed more manly at the time for some reason."

"Visiting Nana." She swatted his arm again. "Very macho."

Jeff's quick one drink had turned into three and a permanent spot at her side. Normally, he wouldn't hit on a woman in a pub, especially the night before a job. But there was something about her—this no-named woman with the curtain of thick brown hair and the feminine giggle that reminded him of springtime. A little voice inside told him to stop stressing and go with it.

"Back to you," he said, loving the way her nose sometimes crinkled when she spoke. "Does your food spilling occur only while traveling?"

She pressed her sexy lips together and laughed at a private memory, making Jeff crazy to know everything about her. "I'm afraid not," she said. "I waited tables in college and I once dumped a whole platter of crab cakes on a woman wearing cashmere."

"Tragic," he said, chuckling at her expression. "Though I'm sure you looked extremely elegant in the process."

She actually snorted a laugh, then put a fist over her mouth and blushed furiously. Jeff hadn't seen anyone so adorably sexy in ages.

"There you go being elegant again." He gave her a wink, causing her to lower her hand and smile, back to looking relaxed. "Which school?"

"Hmm?" She swept her hair off one shoulder, revealing

a mile-long neck. For a moment, Jeff forgot his own question.

"You mentioned you waitressed while at university. I was wondering which school."

Her lips peeled apart, ready to speak, but then didn't right away. "No...I don't think so," she finally replied, fidgeting with the stem of her glass. "Sharing personal information isn't part of tonight's game."

He felt his brows lift. "Is this a game?"

She smiled, letting her eyes lower for a moment and then nodded.

Oh, she's good.

About a dozen scenarios popped into Jeff's mind. All of which required the two of them enjoying much more privacy. "Ahh," he said, returning her smile. "Excellent, I enjoy games. Tell me this, though..." He leaned toward her ear so they were almost cheek to cheek and he could smell her light perfume, graze a strand of her glossy hair. "What exactly are crab cakes? They sound as exotic as you." They were close enough now that he felt her soft breath when she exhaled a laugh.

Of course he knew what crab cakes were. But two could play the mysterious card. After two hours of neither of them disclosing so much as a first name, Jeff knew exactly what game they were playing.

Although, technically, he'd never been a star player in that particular game. Among his mates, he was known as the "relationship guy." What he wanted most from a woman was honesty, someone he could trust, particularly after he'd been burned by the most important person in his life. He hadn't felt that kind of trust in a very long time. Once, he'd had it, but then it shattered beyond repair. Even the memory made his insides clench like a fist, a warning of past mistakes.

No, no relationships. He should focus on chemistry and fun and not worry about putting his heart on the line. For once in his life, he wanted it to be easy—no thinking, just action.

Maybe that was why sitting beside the chatty American with the chocolate-colored eyes felt so right. Every line he sent her, she shot a flirty one right back. This was one damn sexy game. And the way her black dress crept higher up her thigh every time she recrossed her legs put even more privacy-required scenarios in his mind.

"I think Natalie would love a bottle of this wine," she said, as she touched her glass.

"She's a connoisseur?" he asked, running his finger along the rim of her glass, stopping just short of brushing her hand.

"I want to give her something special—and non-Hershey. I hope I remember to call."

Jeff considered asking if she'd like to use his room to make her phone call. He was just one floor up. Then he thought of other reasons to have her in his room. Prone to spilling drinks or not, she didn't seem the type to agree to that. He felt like a player for allowing his imagination to go there.

But every time she laughed at one of his lame jokes or touched his arm, those sexy-time ideas rushed back.

"Well, my internal clock says it's really late," she said, tucking some hair behind both ears.

Jeff felt a wrench of anxiousness at her walking out of his life before he'd even learned her name.

"Actually, it's early. You're in Oz." He pulled back a smile that he hoped was more inviting than nervous. When she locked eyes with him and lifted her own smile, his nerves dissolved. He gazed at her mouth, those full red lips he'd imagined kissing for the last two hours.

Okay, time to cut the crap. Ask for her name, number, Twitter handle, any personal information she was willing to throw his way. He should be a gentleman and stop thinking like one of the predators he studied.

Before he could ask, she tipped her glass, finishing her drink in one gulp, then laid a hand on his thigh. *Well, hello there.* Heat seared from her light touch and shot through his body, causing all gentlemanly intentions to disappear like a stone dropped in the middle of Sydney Harbor.

"You are staying here?" she asked then bit her lip. "I mean, I am, too, but…you have a…a room?"

The question confused him. Or maybe it was the way it was delivered. Despite her very deliberate hand on his leg, she didn't know what she was doing either. Ha! The woman was just as clueless as he was about picking up someone at a pub.

"I do have a room," he confirmed, curious to see what she would do with the information.

She nodded, then slid her hand off his leg and moved off the bar stool. The second her high heels hit the floor, she teetered. Instinctively, Jeff reached out and took her by the waist to steady her. He should suggest they take a walk — they probably both needed fresh air — or maybe they could find a quieter place to continue their conversation.

Before he could suggest either, she fisted the front of his shirt and pulled him forward until their mouths connected. Just like that. Jeff was too caught off guard to react properly. All he could do was dig his fingers into her sides, keeping her close, while keeping himself steady.

Maybe sensing his shock, his mystery woman fiercely broke their kiss, then slapped a hand over her mouth, her brown eyes wide open, like the deed had stunned her more than him.

Jeff tried to speak, but the kiss had left his heart banging against his ribs, harder than the aboriginal clapsticks he'd had when he was a kid.

"I can't believe I did that," she whispered between her fingers.

"I'm very glad you did," he said, feeling the heat of her body as he held her waist. "Takes the pressure off me." She didn't move away. Maybe she didn't really regret the impulsive action. But she didn't make another move toward him, either.

The gentlemanly switch turned on again, reminding Jeff that it wasn't good manners to let her kiss him and not reciprocate.

So he took her hand that was covering her tempting mouth and slid it away, revealing those lips he'd barely had time to taste. He inched his grip around her wrist, then moved her hand to his mouth and kissed it, keeping his eyes locked on hers. He wished he was doing much more than kissing the back of her silky hand, though throwing her on the bar and devouring her like a man-eater wasn't a wise option.

But…he was only human.

Leaning forward, he brushed his mouth over hers. Her lips were soft and warm, parting for him as he went in for kiss number two, which was unbelievably sexy. She rested her body weight against him, wedging herself between his chest and the long bar. When his hand curved low around her hip, he heard her sudden intake of breath and knew he needed to get them somewhere private before he *did* throw her across the bar and they got arrested for public indecency.

With superhuman strength, he pulled his mouth away from hers. She was resting her hands on the tops of his shoulders, her face dipped, but he could hear her ragged, racing breaths, matching his own.

"Tell me if this is too forward," he said in a low voice that was surprisingly shaky, "but do you want to come — "

"*Yes*," she answered, exhaling hot breath on his neck.

He grinned and gave her hip a squeeze. "I must say, this has been the most pleasant surprise I could imagine."

"You're not very imaginative, then." She gave him the flirty eyes. "Good thing I am."

Jeff had no idea what that meant, but wasn't about to miss the chance to find out. He dropped a few bills on the bar, then followed her out of the room. He should've cared that so many eyes watched as they left — after all, he stayed at this hotel whenever he was in town on business, and he was relatively well known with those who bothered to follow his type of career. He was always surprised when someone recognized him as "Great White Cruz" from those spots on the Discovery Channel.

Still, he didn't have the brain power to care who noticed. The blood that should've been flowing to the top portion of his body was tied up elsewhere.

The second they left the noisy pub and rounded the corner toward the lifts, they were unexpectedly alone. Jeff seized the opportunity and pulled her in, locking her mouth into a deeper kiss, really drinking her in — the hint of her last cocktail mixed with flavored lip gloss, the smell of warm skin and moonlight. He cupped the back of her head and she slid her arms around him, her nails scraped across his back. His head swam, completely wrapped up in the moment, loving how she wasn't giving him even a second to think, to reconsider.

This was *so* what he needed.

With their bodies crushed together, he pressed her against the closed lift doors and slid a hand down, exploring her body, stopping at her thigh. She gasped the second his fingers strayed up the inside of her dress. It wasn't his style—all this PDA—but the way she kissed him and clawed him…

When she ran a hand up the front of his shirt, opening two buttons along the way, Jeff's brain snapped awake enough to catch her wrist. "I prefer privacy," he breathed against her cheek. "For many reasons, I don't take my shirt off in front of just anyone."

Her espresso-shaded eyes gazed at him as she reached behind her and pressed the elevator call button. "Give me two minutes," she whispered, her breath labored, "and I'll meet you back here."

"I'm only one floor up," he said, a thumb digging into her hip, the other stroking her lower lip.

She leaned in and kissed his neck. Heat spun from the point on contact down to the pit of his stomach. "Wait for me, Blue Eyes. I'll be right back."

Unable to do much more, Jeff nodded, though he didn't like the idea of her leaving, not even for as little as two minutes, not when he didn't know her name. But it was all part of the challenge, the easiness that came with their game.

So he let go and allowed her to step into the lift. When

she blew him a kiss an instant before the doors slid together, he regretted not jumping in with her and finishing what they'd started—hotel cameras and all. Instead, he clenched both his fists and exhaled a deep growl. Evidently, he'd be practicing patience tonight, as well.

Just like those earlier two hours at the bar had flown by, so did the next two minutes. Two minutes stretched into five, then ten. Jeff had to keep stepping aside to let hotel guests in and out of the lifts.

After twenty minutes passed, he knew he'd been stood up. Though his ego when it came to women was more than healthy, he was surprised how much that stung.

Feeling foolish for about a million damn reasons, he made his way back into the bar, sat in a completely different section and ordered a double. Way too many hours later, he went up to this room. Alone.

Chapter Two

"What's with you this morning?"

Jeff glanced up from the duffel bag containing his wet suit, mask, and fins. He wasn't planning on swimming with his *Carcharodon carcharias* friends, but with an outing like today's, he liked to be prepared for anything.

"Nothing," he said, trying not to snarl at his assistant. "Didn't sleep."

"You look like complete and utter sewer trash, man." Pax had an annoying way with words.

"I'm fine. Ready to get this show on the road." He needed to focus and forget everything about last night. The memory made him feel like an idiot all over again. "Yo, Manny!" he called toward the helm. "What's the holdup, mate?"

Manny made a hand gesture through the window, then left the pilothouse, and walked out onto the deck. "We're not all aboard," he said. "Wouldn't make a very keen captain if I left dock before every passenger arrived."

Jeff glanced around at their down-sized crew. "Who are we waiting for?" he wondered aloud. This was a small, one-day expedition with only a few of Manny's deckhands he'd used dozens of times, plus Manny and Pax. The research would go much quicker with a team this size, which was the whole point.

No fanfare, and thankfully no media.

"Got word last night," Manny said, sliding on a pair of sunglasses. "The uni's sending two more people."

"Who?"

The captain smiled. His teeth gleamed extra white against his coal-dark skin. "Ya not gonna like it."

Jeff felt his stomach muscles tighten. "Who?" he repeated, suspicious of the shit-eating grin on Manny's face. If anyone liked to bust his chops, it was his childhood mate.

Manny cocked his head. "It's audit time, my friend."

"Meaning?"

"Meaning...the head bloke from the science department is sending an accountant to make sure the money they gave you for this project is being spent properly."

Jeff yanked out his cell and pressed speed-dial. "I know what a bloody audit is. I meant, why now? Why today's trip? Don't you think it's a little coincidental — *Sellers*?" he barked into the phone.

There was a pause, then, "Don't say it, Cruz."

The tone of the voice on the other end made Jeff close his eyes, his stomach sinking deeper. It was a done deal. "This is a really bad day to have passengers," he said. "We're all going to be busy and I won't have time to handhold someone through every detail of what I'm doing."

"You're going to have to make the time," Dr. Sellers

replied. They were colleagues, but Jeff knew it was pointless to argue with the head of the department. "The university pays the bills, not you," Sellers said. "We're paying for the use of that boat you're standing on, all your expenses, and every dime that goes into your projects."

Jeff nodded and rubbed the back of his neck. "I know that."

"The budget's tight, and this trip wasn't exactly on the books for so early in the fiscal year."

Now wasn't the time to tell Sellers who was really financing today's outing. The less red tape the better. "Something came up rather quickly," Jeff said. "It's important."

"I figured as much when I saw the request. I'm not doubting its importance, I'm just saying the science department isn't a money tree and this trip shot off red flags. Of course if you allowed a camera crew aboard—"

"No way," Jeff interrupted.

Not that this trip was top secret, but he was trying to keep it on the down low until he knew what they were dealing with. For one thing, it could be dangerous. Or it could end up being a complete bust. Either way, he didn't want the whole thing aired during Shark Week.

His spots on the Discovery Channel had funded many of their expeditions, and Jeff was grateful there was an interest and curiosity about sharks these days. But if he thought one accountant sent from the University of Miami would be a pain in the tail fin, try three cameramen, two sound techs, and a boatload of insurance forms.

"Look, my hands are tied," Sellers said. "I know you hate this, but you're gonna have to find a way to live with it."

Jeff sank onto the leaning post at the side of the boat, feeling the effects of last night's no sleep weighing on him. "Should I even ask who the *other* passenger is?"

A few minutes later—after the news got even worse—they ended the call. Jeff was so frustrated, he felt like throwing his cell into Port Jackson.

"What's the deal?" Pax asked, hooking their two laptop cases straps over his shoulder. "We're seriously being audited today?"

"Looks like it," Jeff confirmed, flatly. "The accountant at an independent firm from the States should be here any minute. Sounds like the uni is covering its ass."

"Manny said we're waiting on two passengers."

"Yeah." Jeff shook his head. "The other's a journo."

Pax's face fell, probably like Jeff's had when he'd heard the news from Sellers. "A reporter? Today?"

"Yep. Not only are we plagued by damn Pricewaterhouse or whatnot, but for all I know, the media will be documenting our every move." He grabbed the back of his already sore neck. "So not what we need today."

"That's what you get for being the poster boy of the shark world," Pax said, probably trying to lighten the mood. "Do they know about Old Faithful?"

Jeff shook his head. "Let's hope not. If our theory's incorrect and Old Faithful isn't even there, no one but us will know this wasn't a routine research cruise."

"Or we could end up making a major discovery, boss."

Jeff couldn't help grinning. "Maybe." Hearing the *clomp* of footsteps, he glanced up the dock into the early morning sunlight to see a kid who looked about twenty heading for the boat.

"This the *Mad Hatter*?" he asked in an American accent.

Manny stepped forward to greet him. "Sure is, son. And you are?"

"Leo. UM sent me for a write-up. University paper, nothing major."

"We've been waiting for you," Manny said. "Come aboard, then. Ain't got all day."

The kid made it up the ladder, then stood on the deck and smiled wide, looking young and eager and well rested. Jeff tried not to hate him on principle—he'd save that for their other "guest."

"Hey...hi," Leo said, probably feeling unwelcomed when no one except Manny did anything but glare at him. "So, great whites, huh?"

"Yeah," Jeff said. "Dangerous bastards. Rip your arms off." He couldn't help smirking when the kid's eyes grew wide; he'd seen that reaction before. Maybe if he could scare him enough to keep him off the boat, one of his problems would be solved. "Sure you're up for this? Trolling for whites isn't for the faint."

"Are you kidding," Leo said. "I freakin' *love* sharks."

Manny tossed his head back and roared with laughter. *Not helping.*

"Just what this boat needs," Pax muttered sarcastically to Jeff. "Jacques Cousteau."

Jeff chuckled bitterly. *Ridiculous.* "I don't have time to stress about it. As long as he and his auditor chum stay out of my way."

"Permission to come aboard?"

Jeff heard the female voice and saw Manny advance double time to the dockside ladder. "And you would be?"

Manny asked.

"Sharona Blaire from SED Independent Auditors of Miami-Dade County. You're the captain of this yacht?"

"*Ship*," Jeff couldn't help correcting under his breath as he turned, ready to begrudgingly greet the other thorn in his side.

"Whoa, steady there," Manny said, as he helped the last addition to the party aboard.

Jeff saw the top of her head first as she climbed up the ladder. Long brown hair next, then the dark eyes that had seemed almost liquidy black by the dim light of the hotel pub. Then he saw those lips he'd kissed…not nearly enough.

His entire body went stiff with shock.

"Oh!" She gasped under her breath when their eyes met across the deck. "Um, hello"—her gaze moved quickly away—"everybody. N-nice day for a sail."

"We use an *engine*," Pax said, using the same condescending tone Jeff had only seconds ago, shooting an elbow into Jeff's ribs. "Landlubber," he tagged on with a sardonic laugh. "This might be fun after all."

"Shut ya gob," Jeff muttered, still unable to move.

"Ms. Blaire." Manny took her arm like the gracious captain he was. "Welcome aboard the *Mad Hatter*."

"Thank you." Her eyes darted back to Jeff's for an instant before Manny went on to introduce her to the other members of the crew.

"Last but not least, this is Dr. Jeff Cruz." He put a hand on Jeff's shoulder. "Our resident marine biologist."

"G'day," Jeff said, looking at her, while trying not to look at her, which was something of a challenge.

"*You're* the leader of this team?" She crossed her arms.

"Funny, I don't remember you mentioning anything about that when — "

"Wait." The kid, Leo, stepped forward, a pen in his hand at the ready. "You two already know each other? Ha-ha... the shark biologist *knows* the auditor sent to shut you down? It's like Romeo and Juliet." He paused to chuckle and pull out a notebook. "That's epic."

Jeff looked at her, incredulous. "Shut us down?"

"No one's shutting anything down," she said, jutting out her chin an inch while gripping the handle of her small wheelie suitcase. "This is a simple audit required by the university. I'm here to do a spot check of how your sponsor's funds are being spent. Purely routine."

"In my experience, there's no such thing as a routine audit," Jeff said. Then he turned to Leo. "And we most certainly do not know each other," he snapped, staring at him first, then flicking his eyes to Sharona, hoping she understood what he was doing and why. "I'm sure she meant she's *heard* about my *research*." Jeff glanced at her again, a bit more imploringly this time. "Am I right, Miss..." He tilted his head. "What did you say your name was?"

"Blaire," Sharona said, lifted her chin, a little annoyed by last night's kissing partner's purposeful dismissal. "Sharona Blaire."

The guy with the backward baseball cap pointed his pencil at her. "Sharona, like the song? Muh-muh-muh-myyy Sharona..." he sang, bobbing his head to the beat.

"Yep, *just* like the song." She glanced at Jeff for a

moment. He was still giving her that intense stare. *Jeez, ease up.* "And no." She waved a hand in the air, trying to appear breezy. "We don't know each other."

It was humiliating enough to remeet the guy she'd almost slept with after knowing him a whopping two hours. When she'd chickened out, she hadn't had the guts to go back down to the bar and tell him why. Instead, she'd hidden in her hotel room and emptied the minibar.

Which is why I'm late at the dock and feeling like reheated crap. What was I thinking?

No matter how irresistible he'd been last night, the man was practically coated in caution tape now. Facing the aftermath of a busted relationship with a coworker was crappy enough—once. No need to get the rep that she was prone to dating on the job. She was on professional thin ice with Garry, anyway, and if it got back that she'd been fraternizing with the person she was supposed to audit, her job—not to mention her reputation—would be toast.

Since their breakup, Garry had become vindictive enough to see to that. Or maybe he'd always treated her that way, like she wasn't important. After they'd been together for months, she'd learned his sister lived less than a mile away…yet he'd never introduced them. She never knew if he'd been thoughtless or simply a hurtful ass. And that had been the first drop in a very deep ocean of douchey behaviors to come.

"So." Sharona folded her arms, not wanting to dwell on her sucky past. "*You're* the famous Dr. Jeff Cruz."

He dipped his chin and exhaled a chuckle, doing a pretty good imitation of laid-back. But she knew better, especially after she'd been a front-row witness to him pinning her against the elevator doors last night. Anything but laid-back. The image was so vivid, her breath caught.

"You're calling yourself famous now?" Manny said, clamping a hand on Jeff's shoulder.

"*Her* words," Jeff said, laying on the humble again, "not mine."

Manny pulled back a toothy grin. "They don't call you *Great White Cruz* for nothing."

Sharona lifted her eyebrows.

"It's just a stupid nickname," Jeff muttered.

"Which you love," Manny jabbed back.

"Shut the—"

Manny's laugh cut him off. "Just messing with ya, mate."

"Impressive to be known as a *great* anything," Sharona offered. Though honestly, she hadn't heard the name Jeff Cruz before reading on her flight about his research being funded by the University of Miami. But she did know men, so why not give his ego a stroke? Despite the short notice and no sleep, she was excited about her assignment, happy to make sure things were fiscally on the up and up with this crew of shark men. That was her only reason for being there.

"I'm Leo." The baseball-cap guy—who looked like a college student—stuck out his hand to shake hers.

"Nice to meet you."

"So, you're with UM, too?"

"No. UM hired me to perform the audit."

"Yeah?" He scribbled in a notebook that seemed to appear out of nowhere. "Would you mind giving me some info about your company?"

"I work for SED and—" Oh, crap. Was he a reporter? First, skating on thin ice at work and then almost hooking up with the leader of the shark guys... Sharona suddenly felt way in over her head.

"Where can I stow my gear?" she blurted, turning to the captain. Manny, was his name—Ngally Manimaliunga—if she recalled Garry's notes correctly.

"There, below." He pointed toward a companionway that probably led to the galley and sleeping quarters.

"Thanks. And I'll need a place to set up my computer here."

Manny gestured to a table and two chairs near the front of the helm, bolted to the deck. "That's all we've got by way of a work station. Inside the helm won't have much extra space."

"This'll be fine," she said. "Thank you." She headed toward the companionway, about to lug her stuff down the ladder, when the space where her bag sat was suddenly empty.

"I've got it," said a low voice at her side. The sound sent a fresh image of last night to the front of her mind. Her mind reminded her body—complete with the phantom feel of Jeff's hot hands low on her hips...which was terribly inconvenient. When she didn't follow, Jeff turned his head and shot her an impatient look that said, *Why are you standing there? Come with me.*

Her heart gave a few hard, jumpy beats but she forced herself to calm down. *Not the time to go stupid swoony again*, she thought. The second they were inside the empty helm, she reached out and grabbed his arm, forcing him to stop.

"I'm sorry," she said in a hushed voice, not wanting anyone aboard the *Mad Hatter* to hear. She did feel she owed Jeff an explanation, though.

*ℒ*OVE *ℬ*ITES

He glanced at her hand resting on his arm, a cold yet blank expression on his face. Not at all like how his blue eyes burned through her last night, begging her wordlessly to go with him, how the touch of his rough lips made her feel like she could burst into flames.

"For what?" he said, indifference coloring his tone.

She blinked, thrown by his coldness. "For last night. For…"

He shrugged and glanced past her shoulder. "I don't know what you're talking about."

Oh? Ohhh, so that's the way he wants to play it. Though I guess he has a right to be pissed.

Sharona quickly removed her hand, and Jeff headed toward the companionway. He got about three paces, then stopped. She braced herself, ready for another hurtful comment hurled her way.

"Sorry," he said after a deep sigh, his back to her.

She blinked, thrown again.

Jeff slowly turned around. "That was—" He cut himself off. Then his blue eyes lifted to hers, just as piercing as last night, making her remember other things from their interchange, then subsequently making her knees wobble. Or maybe it was the sensation of the boat rocking that always made her dizzy.

"Look, what happened, or *didn't* happen," his voice dropped a notch, "it would be very unfortunate if that information were known. It wouldn't do either of us any good."

"I know," she said. *I'm not an idiot.* "I have just as much to lose if this gets out." *Probably way more,* she could have added. "But I can't pretend it didn't happen, either."

He looked at her, his gaze steady, his jaw tight. "Well, that's exactly what we're doing." He pointed toward a narrow doorway. "Lockers down below. Take whichever is empty." Then he walked through the door leading out to the deck.

Bastard.

Chapter Three

As Jeff marched away, he felt like a great white arse. But it was necessary. The second he'd been alone with her, the number of questions that flooded his brain was paralyzing. Number one on the list: *Why did you disappear last night?* And number two: *Was it really some twisted game?*

He wasn't about to ask either. No way. It would've been better if he'd kept up the charade of pretending like he didn't know what she was talking about, hadn't recognize her the second their eyes met...and how his body reacted almost immediately at the sight of her.

He'd tried, but that *brilliant* plan had lasted a whole ten seconds. Yes, she'd ditched him last night without explanation, but he didn't have to be crass. All those boyhood etiquette lessons taught him better. And she'd looked so hurt when he'd said he didn't remember her; like he could forget the way she'd dove into their kiss. It had barely been twelve hours, and he could still feel her soft curves in his hands.

It took everything in him to point her in the direction of the bunks below, then get the hell out of there. Their undeniable chemistry was welcomed last night, but things were very different in the light of day.

"What's up, boss?" Pax asked when Jeff walked out onto the deck. Manny and the other deckhands were readying the ship to undock.

"Nothing," Jeff muttered, sliding his hands in his pockets.

Pax snorted. "Already under your skin."

"Who?"

After Pax nodded in the direction of the cabin, Jeff shook his head and blew out a long breath. *You have no idea*, he felt like saying. "What are you talking about, mate?" he said, kicking a pile of rope over to a corner of the deck.

Pax laughed. "I know it's gonna suck having her aboard today. You're frustrated. I can tell."

"Of course I'm *frustrated*, but not about..." He thrust a hand through his hair. "Never mind." They both turned when the sound of clinking and creaking came from below. Sharona Blaire must be sitting on one of the squeaky bunks. The thought of her and a bed made his chest sting hot, most inopportunely. "Let's get the computers set up."

"We won't be at the spot for an hour."

Jeff didn't care. He needed something to keep his brains and hands busy. "Never too early to prepare," he said, grabbing one of the laptops. "Let's go." They headed into the helm, plugging in under the main control console of the ship. Manny was behind the wheel, steering the *Mad Hatter* away from Sydney and up the coastline.

"Not bad, if you ask me," Manny commented as if they'd been in the middle of a conversation. "Nope, not bad at all."

Jeff glanced at him, figuring what he meant. He'd known Manny a long time; if anyone would see through the charade, it was his oldest friend. "Yep," he muttered, noncommittally, jaw clenched, staring through the glass toward the clear, morning sky.

Manny chuckled. "Whatever, mate. Did you see her legs? What I could do with those stems."

Jeff tried to ignore how his blood started to boil. Why was he feeling territorial over a woman he hadn't even known the name of until a few minutes ago? Sharona. What the hell kind of dead-sexy name was that?

"I didn't notice her legs," he lied. After her eyes, lips, and curves, her long legs were the next place Jeff's eyes had settled when she'd stepped aboard the ship. Why the bloody hell was she wearing formfitting khaki shorts like she was going on safari?

"For all I care, she's just a passenger," he added, almost laughing at his unconvincing tone.

Pax took the seat next to him and opened their second laptop. "Boss is nothing but focused on today's agenda, Cap," he said, like the loyal assistant he was. "When he's motivated like this…" He whistled. "The woman could walk around buck naked and he wouldn't notice."

Jeff struck the wrong key, nearly deleting the chart on his screen. Sharona in the nuddy. Damn it, he'd have a devil of a time getting that image out of his head.

Maybe it had been a blessing in disguise that she'd never come back last night. If they'd gone through with what they'd both wanted, how the hell would he be able to concentrate today? The memory of her kiss and his hands on her body was bad enough.

"What's all this?" Sharona asked as she emerged into the room.

Again, Jeff's fingers tripped over themselves on the keyboard, as he caught a whiff of her perfume or hand lotion. All flowery and sexy. He wondered how an elegant woman like that would smell in the roughest Outback or after a few days at sea. He'd always loved the hint of salt water on skin. He was sure Sharona would smell even sexier. But that was *not* where his thoughts should be.

He'd mixed business with pleasure once, and that resulted in the biggest mistake of his life. Jeff had fully trusted very few people since then. Only a handful with work and exactly zero with his heart.

"Technical stuff," Pax said to Sharona, tilting the screen of his computer away from her. "You wouldn't understand."

"Would you mind explaining it to me?" She pulled out a computer tablet and swiped a finger across it. "It's why I'm here."

She came around to stand on the other side of Jeff, probably sensing that Pax was being overly protective. He should applaud the behavior and do the same thing. He hated people snooping around his job, throwing up unnecessary road blocks. Asking too many questions.

But he'd already been rude to her. It wasn't her fault that she was the one woman in the world who he could not have any kind of relationship with. Of course, as dumb luck would have it, she was also the one woman in the world who stirred something in him he'd thought was dead.

"This here," he pointed at the computer, "is a Macbook." He was going for charm. That usually worked when he wanted someone off his back. *Sharona on her back, however…has a nice ring.*

"Hilarious." She rolled her eyes, loosening up. "I've got a list of items I'd like to go through with you. I know how much they cost to buy and repair, but I'll need to understand their importance and significance. For example…" She swiped a finger across her tablet again. "What is the Bose Nautical Sonar LX?"

One of the most complicated pieces of equipment we have aboard, he wanted to say. *So don't touch it.* "In layman's terms," he said instead, after a deep breath, "it measures sound against movement under water."

"What is its necessity in regards to this project?"

She slid on a pair of reading glasses, looking not only sexy but smart.

"What do you know about this part of the ocean?" he asked.

She didn't reply for a moment. "Well, from what I understand, it's deep. Past the reef and up the coastline, it drops off. Isn't that where the sharks…"

Jeff nodded. "Yes, where we're going is a common area for great whites." He swiveled around in his chair to face her. "They love cool, deep water. And murky. Hard to track when they go farther than a certain depth. We need special equipment."

"I see." She typed with one finger while chewing her bottom lip. "Deep water," she said like she was talking to herself.

"They love warm, shallow water, too," he added. "In fact, sharks can be found in just about any body of water at any time of year. They're pretty much unavoidable."

He noticed her shudder. "Do you have a problem with

sharks, Ms. Blaire?"

She held her tablet close to her chest and started twirling the rings on her fingers. She had three on each hand; she'd worn none last night. "I'll admit it's an irrational fear. I blame Peter Benchely."

Jeff couldn't help smiling. "I reckon he did give sharks an unfair rep."

She nodded and wrapped her arms around herself. Jeff felt the desire to hold her and protect her from whatever made her afraid. Where had that come from?

Pax started to laugh, mockingly. "You're afraid of *sharks*?" he said. "Better wear a life jacket, then. Not that it'll do much good." He closed his computer, grinned at her, then walked out onto the deck, humming the theme song to *Jaws* as he left.

Jeff felt like punching him. Those movies weren't the only culprits for giving great whites a bad name.

"Sharks are like any other creature," he said to her. "They're on this planet to live and thrive in their own territory. It's only when man started infringing on that territory that the troubles began. If someone broke into your house, wouldn't your instinct be to protect it?"

"I don't have rows of razor-sharp teeth, a double-jointed jaw, and speeds up to twenty-five miles per hour," she pointed out.

Jeff wanted to laugh. At least she knew a thing or two about great whites. "I guess I'm lucky you don't."

She pushed her glasses up on her nose. "I don't plan on getting anywhere near them," she added. "I'll be fine as long as I can keep my equilibrium under control. I sometimes get a little…seasick."

"Yet you took an assignment that puts you in open ocean?"

She turned to stare out the window. "That's a long story."

She was being intriguing again. Like last night. Mysterious. Jeff didn't like that. Then again, he *really* liked it.

Unable to control his curiosity, he asked, "So you didn't volunteer for this job?"

"I'm sent where I'm needed," she said but then began worrying on her bottom lip. "Actually, I *did* ask for the next assignment that required travel." She waved a hand through the air. "Another long story; personal stuff." She glanced at him and lifted an eyebrow. "I don't do personal."

He nodded, remembering that about her from last night.

Sharona went back to her tablet and asked Jeff about a few more pieces of equipment, what they were used for and if she could see them later. He did his best to give the bare minimum information. Despite his annoying attraction toward her, he didn't know this woman, and was not going to divulge more than necessary.

"And what are all these dots?" She pointed at his computer screen.

"Part of a control group."

She pulled back her pointing finger like she was afraid of being shocked. Or *bit*. "Sharks, you mean."

Jeff nodded, again intrigued as to why she was here... why she'd taken a job that put her on the water if she was afraid of sharks and got seasick.

"O-oh." She swallowed and seemed to shrink back a bit.

"These are the animals we've been tracking the last few years." Jeff pointed at each of the seven dots on the screen, getting nearer the farther up the coast they went. "We know they've come back to this part of the ocean."

"Tracking?" she asked, tapping on her tablet. "How, exactly? I don't recall seeing tracking devices on my list."

Jeff tried not to groan aloud. *She's just doing her job*, he thought. It was a nice reminder that he should not be wondering if her red lip gloss was the same flavor she was wearing last night. Strawberry.

"We attached a sensor to the dorsal fin. May I see your list?"

Sharona met his eye, her fingers curling around her tablet. "Why?"

"If you can't find it on your list, it might be labeled differently." This wasn't exactly true, but he did want a look at that list. He held out his hand. "Do you mind?"

After a pause, she exhaled and handed it over. The list was extensive. He probably didn't have such a detailed inventory back home at the lab. He ran a finger over the face, flipping pages. "This is one of the older trackers," he said, handing it back. "A box of them is stowed below."

"Thanks." She entered something into her database. "You mentioned attaching them to the dorsal fin. How?"

"Is that part of your audit?"

She shrugged and removed her glasses. "No, but I'm curious."

"Scientists have been doing it for decades. There're many ways to do it. Most common is a kind of combination between a dart and a hole punch."

Sharona lowered her tablet and gaped at him. "That sounds brutal."

"Actually, it's not. The dorsal fin is almost 100 percent cartilage, not many nerves. The initial insertion is a shock to them, but after a few seconds, they don't seem to notice it."

"*Seem*?" She repeated his word, though her tone was filled with skepticism. "They're helpless animals and you come at them with a spear?"

"They're hardly helpless." He laughed. "Don't tell me you work for PETA in your spare time?"

She blinked and gazed toward the water. "Well, no. I just care."

So do I, Jeff was about to reply, but was cut off.

"You say they don't feel it, but how could you possibly know?"

"Because I've been studying them for a very long time. And before me, others have. It irritates them initially, sure, but it's by no means brutal."

She folded her arms. "Says you."

Grrr! Why was her sassy attitude turning him on rather than off? He felt like kissing her just to shut her glossy mouth.

"Look," he said, crossing his arms so he would have something to do with his hands. "There's no law against how we track these fish. Not in Australia, and not in international waters. You're here to do an audit on how I'm spending the uni's money—fine." He pushed back his chair to stand. "But if you think you're going to catch me doing something inhumane, Sharona Blaire, plan on a very boring day."

He shut his laptop and walked out to the deck to stand in the sun, annoyed with her but mostly with himself.

A hole-punch? If that wasn't the definition of inhumane, she didn't know what was. The blue-eyed man she'd met last night had been so charming and gentle. Was that all an act to get her naked? Working closely with Garry and other biology research teams, she'd known a few scientists who were all about making the next discovery—no matter what the cost to nature. Sharona couldn't help feeling disappointed that Jeff Cruz was like that, too.

From her place inside the helm, she watched him through the glass. The ocean wind blew through his short dark hair. She noted the broadness of his shoulders. She'd noticed them last night, too. Had even felt them through his shirt—how muscly they were and how sturdy and strong. He'd been dressed up last night, looking crisp and sharp in a white shirt and pressed pants. Today, he was all casual, and—much to her chagrin—he looked even hotter. Probably because he was more at home on a boat than on land.

And why was *that* completely sexy?

He wore a dark blue T-shirt that brought out the color of his eyes when he turned her way. It could've been the light in the bar last night, but she hadn't realized how tan he was. Maybe from having a career that kept him outdoors. His faded jeans gave her eyes many angles of interest.

"He's not usually so abrupt."

Sharona forgot Manny was a few feet away, trimming the mainsail or battening down the hatches or whatever captains did. Her experience on the water was pretty slim—unless you counted the swimming pool at her condo—and she knew even less about the workings of a ship the size of the *Mad Hatter*.

She cursed herself for not spending more time studying up on nautical life. Then again, if she hadn't ventured to the bar last night, she wouldn't have met Jeff or kissed him and felt so alive and brave and wanted all in the space of two hours. She'd needed that…to drum up the courage to make the first move on him. If nothing else, he'd helped her bust out of the comfort zone she'd been trapped in ever since breaking off her engagement. Because of Jeff, she knew passion was still alive in her, and she was grateful for that.

Too bad there couldn't be anything more, not with what she was there to do. It was a pretty glaring conflict of interest. Plus, he lived in Australia and she obviously didn't. Weren't relationships hard enough without putting a twenty-hour plane ride between you? She bit her lip and set her gaze on him again.

"Was he abrupt?" she said, turning to smile at Manny, who was smiling back even wider.

Jeff was suntanned, but Manny was dark. He had a different kind of accent, too. Musical. It made everything he said sound jokey.

"You being here was a surprise to him," he said, hitting a button on the console. The boat's engine made a revving sound and took on speed.

At the sudden motion, she exhaled a tiny squeak, then gripped the ledge on the front of the console. "I was surprised, too," she admitted.

Manny's eyebrows lifted. "So you *do* know each other?"

Her heart slammed. "Um…no, I…I meant—"

"Yeah." Manny grinned, turning his gaze forward, a victorious smile on his mouth. "I thought so."

Crap. "Please," she whispered urgently. "We *don't* really know each other. We kind of met at the hotel, and before that, there was all that turbulence in first class and the

Bloody Mary, but that's *all*." She glanced out the window at Jeff. He was talking to Pax, near the edge of the boat on the right-hand side. Starboard bow, she reminded herself.

Just then, Leo the reporter walked out on the deck and joined the other two. She shook her head. "Needless to say," she continued to Manny, "it wouldn't do Dr. Cruz or myself any good if that information were known. As innocent as it sounds."

"As *confusing* as it sounds." Manny chuckled. "Don't worry, I shall be as quiet as the Outback on a Sunday."

Sharona exhaled slowly, feeling the muscles in her shoulders release. Though she didn't completely understand his reference, she decided to believe Manny and not stress.

"Thank you," she said. "This has turned into an awkward assignment for everyone, I'm afraid. I didn't mind taking a last-minute trip to Australia—it's beautiful country. But my boss was kind of hasty about it. Which is typical, I guess, considering our history." She felt Manny's piercing black eyes on her. "To tell the truth, we used to be a couple—engaged."

"You're not anymore?"

She shook her head. "But I really believe in what we do. I know people think auditors are the bad guys trying to thwart progress, but that's not what I'm doing. I'm here to help. More often than not, I've found ways to save researchers money and I'd like to think we're all on the same team and—"

She took a breath when Manny's laugh cut her off.

"What?"

"You sound as passionate as Cruz." He glanced at her for a quick second. "You two are more alike than he knows,

I reckon."

Seriously doubtful, she thought.

Sharona asked Manny a few questions about the mechanics of the ship and he even managed to help check off some items on her list. "Thanks again," she said and slid her tablet and glasses into her bag and blew out a breath, mentally preparing for the first true test of her sea legs.

The air felt warm and the wind was crisp. She took a deep inhale, trying to get used to the stingy smell of ocean. The rubber soles of her shoes gripped the deck. It was a good thing she'd Googled the proper ship footwear before she'd left home. Her usual strappy sandals would have sent her overboard.

She walked toward the unoccupied foredeck. When she stood still, it was kind of a rush, how the waves kicked up spray, shooting up the occasional splash. Only a few times did she find herself teetering.

Hold on, stomach, she pleaded. *Be a good girl for me today.*

"I hope you're not waiting for someone to hold you from behind and declare 'I'm the king of the world.'"

Sharona couldn't help laughing, as Jeff came up beside her. "That movie always bugged me," she admitted, happy for the distraction from the rocking waves.

"Reckon you better not let *him* hear that." He nodded toward Leo.

Another giggle escaped her lips. "So it's not *only* last night that you're charming. I wondered if I'd imagined that."

He cocked a brow, looking exactly as he had in the bar when he'd met her eye over their drinks. "Not everything changes when the sun comes up," he said in a low voice.

For a second, she hoped she was finally getting the chance to explain what had happened last night...that her chickening out had nothing to do with him. But the moment disappeared when Jeff jerked his head to the side as one of the deckhands approached from behind.

"Yeah," Sharona replied, feeling weighed down and deflated. "Um, would you mind telling me what those are for?" she asked, gesturing at a box that Pax was unloading.

"They're cameras."

She rolled her eyes. "I know they're cameras. There are ten on the audit list. Are they all used?"

Jeff rubbed his stubbled yet firm jaw, not answering right away. "We're here mostly as observers."

"Okay," she said, pulling out her tablet to make a note. "That's what I was told when I was assigned this, but I have to think there's more. Especially since Garry—he's my boss—was hell-bent on me dropping everything and catching the first flight to Sydney."

"I can't imagine why he's so curious about what we're doing today."

"*Right.*" Sharona didn't know Jeff very well, but she knew he was holding something back. He had the same look in his eyes now that he'd had last night when he'd kissed her, pulled away for a second, then *really* kissed her. *Yes, definitely holding back.*

She was about to demand to know what he was trying to hide when Jeff said, "Do you know anything about these animals?"

"Um." She looked down at her tablet, like it might just happen to contain a shark glossary. "Not a whole lot."

He leaned on the gunwale running along the inside edge.

"For starters, they're one of the most mysterious creatures on the planet. Particularly great whites. Because they're so difficult to track, we don't know a lot about their patterns. Technology's grown exponentially over the last decade, so we're learning more now than ever."

"That's exciting," Sharona said.

Jeff lifted his eyebrows. "You think so?"

She sighed in exasperation. "Look, just because I was sent here to make sure funds aren't being misspent doesn't mean I don't believe in science and progress. Because I *do*."

She hated the way her voice rose to that shrill level that always happened when she got overly emotional. Nonetheless, she did *not* like the idea of anyone spearing anything through its fin.

"Nice speech," Jeff said. His voice had a hint of respect in it. Also a hint of amusement. She didn't like not being taken seriously, either.

"So?" She waved a hand. "Continue."

"Right." He ran a hand through his dark hair and looked toward the oncoming waves. "One of the most elusive things about the white shark is their, uh…" His eyes moved to hers and he held them there.

"Their what?" she asked when he didn't finish, a bit rapt by his expression.

He kept his eyes locked on her. "Their mating."

"Mating," she repeated, feeling a flutter in her stomach at the way he was looking at her…then suddenly *not* looking at her.

"We don't know if individual animals spawn in a certain spot every time—kind of like a human might go to a particular *pub* if she wants some action. Just an example, mind you."

She folded her arm, feeing her cheeks heat up. "Pub. Uh-huh."

Jeff leaned against the railing, his expression looking smug at her embarrassment. "For all we know, sharks are just, ya know, doing it everywhere."

"Like the Kardashians?"

He stared at her for a beat, then that tight expression relaxed into a smile as he slid his hands into his jean pockets. "And probably just as reckless," he said. "Or so I'd like to think. That's one of the reasons we're intrigued about why we've tracked these sharks back here. The gestation period is twelve-to-eighteen months. It's been about that long since we last saw them in these waters."

"You're thinking this could be like a favorite pub for sharks? A mating ground?"

"Dunno. But it's certainly worth finding out, don't you think?"

"Have you ever seen two sharks doing…?" She shrugged. "You know."

"It's extremely rare." His accent had grown heavy as he leaned forward, his arm brushing hers. Goose bumps broke out across her skin. "But who knows. Maybe, if we play just the right mood music, you and I will get lucky, Sharona Blaire."

Was he talking about shark reproduction…or human? And…was he flirting? Earlier, he'd gone cold and hostile when she'd tried to apologize. The man was a ball of contradiction. A very sexy, very nice-smelling contradiction.

"Well." She swallowed, staring into his eyes. "I'm all for getting lucky."

Chapter Four

It was like a spell was broken the second Pax called his name from across the boat, shaking him awake. He hadn't meant to talk about sex—marine or not—with Sharona. Since the second they'd met, she brought out the cheesy singles bar in him. They'd been on the boat for an hour and he'd already imagined kissing her a million different ways and on a million parts of her body.

If he didn't keep his head in the game, today would go to shit.

"Yeah, Pax. What is it?" he asked, after breathing out a long exhale and stepping away from the tantalizing bait at his side.

"Got our first sighting. They're faint but…"

Jeff sent one glance Sharona's way then strode to where Pax stood by the side, pointing toward the water.

"See."

"I'll be damned," he said, catching a quick sight of the

telltale black triangle along the horizon. "How far?"

"Kilometer and a half, I'd wager."

"Close enough." Jeff felt a healthy shot of adrenaline in his blood. "Manny!" he called toward the helm. "Drop anchor."

"You got it," Manny returned. The noises of the engines cut.

"What's happening?" Sharona was suddenly at his side, looking a little pale, a little green, too. Was she seasick already? "Why are we stopping?"

"That's why." Pax was pointing dead ahead.

Sharona squinted into the sun, shading her eyes like a sun visor. "I don't see anything."

Jeff moved to stand behind her, rested his hands on top of her shoulders, and lowered his face so their cheeks touched. "There," he said, moving her to angle in the correct direction. He could tell she was holding her breath, because he both heard and felt when she finally inhaled and her breath hitched. It had hitched in exactly the same way last night after she'd first kissed him.

At the memory, he dropped his hands, stepped back, and cleared his throat. "See it now?"

She nodded but didn't look at him. "Um, yeah. The black fin?"

"It's coming this way," Pax said. "Lemme check the database to see if it's one of—yep." He gestured at the computer screen. "Jeff, mate, she's one of our females."

Jeff grinned, another boost of adrenaline hitting. "Which one?"

Pax consulted the screen for a moment. "Matilda."

"Waltzing Matilda." Jeff remembered this one. She wasn't the largest female he'd ever tagged, but man was she feisty. He dug feisty—in sharks and in women. He tried not to recall the sexy way Sharona had pulled him into that first kiss last night. Talk about aggressive. "You got her on the monitor, Pax?" he forced himself to say.

"Sure do," Pax replied. "Here she comes."

Sharona made quick notes about the three unopened boxes outside the helm and a small recycling receptacle that looked like it had never been used. She'd ask about those later because, due to the sudden excitement of the crew—the sighting of Waltzing Matilda was huge news. From what she'd read about the purpose of this research trip, they were retrieving information from tags.

But what kind of tag? And would she be able to get a look at one? More importantly, how the hell did they plan on getting something off the dorsal fin of a moving great white shark? Flashes of that scene from *Jaws* when the shark ate half a fishing boat and all of Robert Shaw popped into her mind. But that was only a movie, right?

This was way above her pay grade.

Once the anchor dropped, the big ship slowed, then stopped, rocking back and forth. Sharona's stomach rolled with the waves, and she gripped the railing, trying to steady both her legs and stomach. She was not about to miss seeing her first shark in the wild because she was blowing chunks overboard.

"Look!" one of the crew shouted.

Everyone rushed to the other side, staring out at the distance. She glanced at Jeff, who was also at the railing.

As she gingerly crossed the deck like a newborn colt, she wondered if it would be totally inappropriate to ask Jeff to point her in the right direction again.

Yeah, that had been very nice, the way he'd slid in, his strong, solid body taking up the space behind her, the touch of his cheek against hers, his big hands on her shoulders. Her thoughts had instantly drifted to their moments outside the elevator, those same hands wandering up the inside of her dress.

"Here she comes—whoa!" Jeff was obviously keeping his mind on work, which was what Sharona should've been doing, too.

Why was this man such a distraction?

With careful steps, she moved down the side of the ship, sliding in beside two deckhands, who were paying no attention to her, but at something in the water twenty feet out. One of the other guys threw something overboard. Whatever it was sank but it was attached to an orange buoy.

Buoys… Dozens of those were on her audit list. But now was not the time to consult the database. If she accidentally dropped her iPad in the water, Garry would make her pay for it. She let go of the railing long enough to make sure the bag holding her tablet was strapped securely across her shoulder, then she shaded her eyes and gazed out to sea in the same direction as the others.

She could make out only the fin, which was moving toward the boat at a pretty fast clip. It was hard to see anything below the surface, but after a few seconds, her focus adjusted. At first she thought it was a shadow overhead, of something huge…like a small airplane? But then she noticed the aerodynamic head, then…about mile behind that…the tail.

The damn thing had to be fifteen feet long. And coming straight at them like a torpedo.

All she heard was the excited exclamations of the guys on either side of her at the railing. All she felt was a confused kind of heavy buzz inside her head. All she saw were teeth.

The analytical part of her brain understood that the boat wasn't suddenly rocking on top of the waves, but that the momentum and wake of the two-ton animal breaking surface, then veering away, gave the *sensation* of rocking up and down…and up and down…up and down. Or maybe *she* was rocking. Either way, it was a perfect storm.

With one hand, she grabbed her stomach, then grasped the railing with her other hand, only halfway aware of the string of curse words flying from her mouth. Many of which her Navy SEAL brother would be proud of.

She shut her eyes, hoping to calm the internal tidal wave of nausea, and bent forward to lay her forehead on the railing, groaning aloud. Through the haze of queasiness, she didn't realize she was hanging onto the railing with a death grip until she was being pried away.

"Don't touch me," she tried to say.

"Hey." She heard a soft voice but didn't know where it was coming from. "Let go." Someone was peeling her fingers off the railing, then she felt an arm around her as she was being pulled from the edge. Without thinking, she leaned in and clung to the front of the shirt, allowing her wobbly legs to be half dragged away.

Within a few steps of walking into the cooling breeze, she felt better, though her head still hammered hard behind her ears. The next thing she knew, the bright sunlight was shaded and she was propped against a wall.

"You're safe."

She blinked once, then forced her gaze to focus on the pair of intense blue eyes staring back at her, brows arched in concern.

Jeff reached out and pressed his palm to her cheek. "Just breathe," he said, soothingly, running a thumb across her skin. "Hey…there you are." A corner of his mouth pulled back into a real smile, the first she'd seen on him today. "You okay?"

"Yeah," she said after a swallow, noting the quiver in her voice. Her head was still pretty fuzzy, too. "What was that?"

"I think you were going into shock." He tilted his head like he was examining her from another angle. "Still might be, I'm afraid."

"It's not *shock*. It's my…" She didn't speak the word but pressed a hand against her stomach in pantomime.

"Your first time seeing a shark breech? Wasn't she a beaut?"

"You could say that." Her pulse was thrumming behind her ears so she closed her eyes, trying to stop the imagined rocking of the heavy boat. *Seasickness is all in your mind,* she inwardly chanted. *Give it a second and it'll pass.*

Jeff shifted his weight, and she felt his thumbs stroke across her cheeks. "Sharona, it's okay. You're in a ship surrounded by eight hundred tons of steel."

Please don't talk about the boat…

"Matilda is in the water. *Outside*. You're safe."

She opened her eyes and looked at him. Why was he explaining that to her? Yes, she had a normal fear of sharks, completely illogical and unfounded, of course, fueled by bad movies on the SyFy channel with fake blood and guts and…

Not good.

Inadvertently, she clamped her eyes shut and jolted in a full-body shudder. It was like she was being choked from the inside; oxygen couldn't reach her lungs like it should. But at least she wasn't nauseous anymore.

Jeff's body moved closer, both hands cradling her cheeks. "You're moaning again." His voice was lower and closer than before. "Stay with me." She felt his breath fanning her face, soft like a breeze off the ocean, such a nice, gentle breeze.

The next second, his lips crashed against hers.

If there had been air in her lungs, she wouldn't have known what to do with it. He kissed her fiercely, making her head spin wilder than a whirlpool, knocking every last puff of breath from her body. His hands slid down the sides of her neck and she swayed back, only to find she was being steadied by the steel wall of the helm.

At the first break in their kiss, she sucked in an audible gulp of air, then grabbed the front of his shirt, pulling him in. As one of his hands cradled the back of her head, the other pressed into the small of her back. Her heart pounded, faster even than when she'd seen Matilda in the flesh.

Jeff pulled back, but only to move to her jaw, his mouth trailing to her ear, sending sizzles of pleasure up and down her spine. She released her grip on his shirt to slip her arms around him, palming the hard muscles along the way. His breath tickled her ear as he rested his lips on her hairline. Traces of last night's cologne and today's sunshine on his skin awakened a new hunger. She arched toward him, needing to be closer, needing his lips on hers like she needed air.

"Good. You're breathing again."

"Again?" she whispered, lifting up on her toes.

When Jeff moved his face away, her skin felt cold,

missing the sunny warmth that accompanied him. She peeled her eyelids apart, focusing on his blue eyes. They weren't watching her with that intense concern anymore. He actually looked…cocky. That Han Solo crooked grin.

"You'd stopped for a minute," he explained. "Before."

Her heart was racing too fast now; she didn't understand what he meant. Stopped? Why had she stopped breathing? And what did that have to do with him stopping in the middle of their kiss? Was he trying to get back at her for last night?

"You appear to be breathing fine now," he added. Humor colored his thick, sex-on-a-stick accent. "Though, maybe a little…heavier than normal."

Heat rose to her cheeks when she noticed how loud and jagged her breathing was.

"Sorry," he said, moving back another few inches. "I thought you could use a shock to the system. You were losing it there for a minute."

And the hits keep on coming.

"You thought I was about to faint?" she asked, wishing she were at the bottom of the Pacific.

"As I just explained, you weren't breathing, so — "

"And that was your idea of mouth to mouth?" She lifted an eyebrow. "Do you do that every time a member of your crew is about to pass out?"

Jeff laughed, and let his arms drop to his sides. "I'm no MD, but I've always been good at…thinking on my feet." The way his eyes flashed to her mouth made her blush all over again. "Did you call Natalie?"

"What?"

"Last night, you mentioned…" He paused to lower his voice. "You said it was your best friend's birthday and you were reminding yourself to call her." He tilted his head. "Though you were also confused about the time difference, afraid you'd missed her birthday."

A gush of warmth washed over her. Of all the things they'd talked about last night, this was what he remembered. It was one of the things she'd liked about him—he listened, he was thoughtful. So many of the good-looking men she'd met lately skipped over honing that personality trait.

But not Blue Eyes from the bar last night.

Not Jeff Cruz, the guy standing in front of her now. The guy who'd kissed her completely breathless once, then kissed her again so she *could* breathe.

"I haven't called Nat," she admitted, allowing a tiny part of her brain to feel guilty about that, while the rest of her brain was doing its best to keep her hands from tearing off Jeff's T-shirt so she could get a look at that firm chest she'd been pressed against. "When we get back tonight, I will. Thanks for the reminder."

"You're welcome," he said, lifting a smile that made her toes curl. "Let me grab you some water. Don't move." His big, capable hands—that had been holding her face just moments ago—gently swayed her so her back rested against the wall. Then he disappeared around a corner. She was glad she had the wall to rest against; otherwise, she was quite sure her knees would buckle to the floor.

Medicinal or not, in her whole life she'd never been kissed like that.

Despite the obvious complications of their jobs and her craptastic split with Garry and the small fact that Dr. Great White Han Solo Jeff Cruz could be such an *ass*...she wanted him to kiss her like that again.

Chapter Five

"Damn it, Cruz," Jeff muttered under his breath. "Cool the hell off."

He needed a stiff drink before he dared return to Sharona. What a line: *I'm no MD, but...* Rubbish! He'd fantasized about kissing her ever since she'd climbed the ladder.

Logic screamed that he should keep away from her for the rest of the day—he'd tried, but when he'd heard the swearing, saw how paper-pale she'd turned the second Matilda sailed under the ship, the instinct to protect her took over.

He opened the galley fridge and pulled out a water.

Though he hadn't planned on kissing her as a health precaution, she truly did look on the brink of passing out. Hadn't he read somewhere that it's good to distract the thoughts of a person who is about to go into shock?

Maybe it was a screwed up move, and he wouldn't have

let the kiss continue if Sharona hadn't responded the way she had. She'd seemed surprised at first, much as Jeff had been surprised when she'd grabbed him at the pub.

He leaned a shoulder against the wall, smiling at the memory. Bloody hell, that had been sexy. The mere recall made his internal temperature climb higher than the Great Victoria Desert in summer. Last night had been about the rush of no-strings sex, but seeing her today turned logic on its head. Now, he imagined reaching out to hold her hand, to listen to her talk about her friends, to take her on dates. To bring her home.

But none of that could be. Even if they could figure out a way for a research scientist and a not-for-profit auditor to be together, her home wasn't his home and Jeff could never do the long-distance thing…despite how much he wanted to bolt to her and finish that kiss.

He'd meant his kiss to be therapeutic, the kinder equivalency of a slap. But, he liked kissing Sharona Blaire, a lot—he never wanted to stop. He loved the touch of her soft skin and the way she'd held on so tightly like she truly needed him. He hadn't felt needed in ages. Most of the women he'd been with made it clear they didn't need anybody. Including his ex-wife. Which had been only one of their problems.

Maybe it was his macho instinct, but if Jeff ever did fall in love again, he wanted a woman who needed him as much as she loved him. Could he ever find that?

He quickly drained his own bottle of water and grabbed another for Sharona. When he rounded the corner toward the companionway, she was standing right where he'd left her. Almost like she was waiting for them to pick up where they left off.

Jeff couldn't force his brain to think of anything he'd rather do than roughly pin that gorgeous body against the wall then take his sweet time.

If only…

"Here," he said, handing her the water.

"Thank you." She placed the iced-down bottle to her cheek. Cooling herself off. Jeff swallowed, staring at her dark eyes, her perfect, flushing skin.

"You're supposed to drink it," he said. "I'm a non-MD, remember?"

Sharona exhaled a breathy laugh, then twisted off the cap and took a deep drink, her full, lips puckering. He'd never been so jealous of a water bottle.

"Thanks," she said after a few deep breaths. "Again, for your…um, help."

He couldn't help smiling, rubbing the back of his neck. "No worries."

She took one more drink and gazed up at him much the same way she had right before she'd kissed him last night.

"About that, though," he blurted. "It was an emergency action." He ran a hand through his hair. "It would be a bad idea if it happened again."

When she sighed, he knew she understood. It did make him slightly happy that she looked disappointed.

"I know," she said, folding her arms across her chest. "We're both here to do a job, and not…anything else."

At least they were on the same page, though Jeff also knew he was fooling himself. Sharona Blaire had crept into his heart. As a scientist, he knew his curiosity couldn't rest until he figured out why.

"Jeff?" she said, her teeth catching on her bottom lip as

she spoke his name.

Fascinating.

"Yeah?"

"I think they need you out there." She tilted her head, pointing out.

"Cruz! Come on, mate, time to roll."

Jeff blinked at the sound of Pax's voice and gave himself a mental head thwap, needing to shock himself back to reality. Hmm, maybe he should suggest another kiss…

Focus, Cruz!

He was aboard the *Mad Hatter*, doing possibly the most important research of his career, and all he wanted to do was snog this woman in the corner like a teenager.

"Yeah, on my way!" he called back. He stepped away and glanced at her one last time. "You're okay?"

She nodded. "All better. I'll catch up in a minute."

He lifted his eyebrows, fighting the urge to reach out and cradle her chin. "You should probably take it easy for a while."

"I'm halfway done with the inventory," she said, grabbing her bag. She took one last sip of water, then smiled. "Besides that, I don't want to miss seeing the *famous* Jeff Cruz in action."

Dang stupid weak stomach, and dang stupid job! Sharona thought as she watched Jeff walk away. The way his jeans clung to his perfect butt, the one she'd been inches away from exploring.

Why was life so unfair that the one guy she felt

uncontrollable chemistry with—even when they weren't even touching—was the only guy she had to keep her hands off?

She took a moment to straighten her clothes, making sure Jeff's skilled hands hadn't undone anything that should have been done. Then she fingered her hair into a ponytail, allowing the sea breeze to touch her still-flushing neck. Only after sufficiently cooling off did she step into the bright sunshine.

Most of the crew was gathered at the bow. Jeff was there, gesturing at the screen of a laptop. "She broke surface three times," he said. "That should give us additional data from the satellite."

Sharona moved into the huddle and drew out her tablet. Just from listening to the conversation between Jeff and the rest of the crew, she was able to ascertain a lot about a few of the items on her list. She was checking off much faster than anticipated. Hopefully Jeff would be able to help her knock off the list before he got really busy.

"Feeling better?" Leo said.

"Much," she replied, glancing toward Jeff. "He gave me a…a drink. Yes, much better."

"So…" He leaned against the railing. "What do you make of this?"

"Of what?"

He nodded in the general direction of the crew. "The research they're working on. All this talk about new technology. It's still untested."

"I didn't hear about any new technology."

Leo stared at her. "That's kind of the whole point of this trip. To test the trackers."

Sharona's job wasn't to report back to Garry about Jeff's

research, but what Leo said made her suspicious. "Is that why *you're* here?" she asked. "Why exactly did UM send you?"

Leo shrugged. "I happened to be in Sydney and someone from the science department contacted me."

"That's pretty coincidental."

"Not really," Leo said after a few moments. "Thing is — and this is between you and me — I was hired by SED…same as you."

She stared at him. "Garry Cook sent you here?"

Leo nodded.

"So you're not a reporter for UM?"

"I am, but…"

"But you're undercover, reporting *for* him." She considered that for a moment, then scoffed. "Classic Garry dick move," she muttered. "You say there's new technology aboard. I'm sure Garry's *dying* to find out what it is." She looked at Leo. "Have you learned anything? What are you going to report?"

"I don't know yet."

She was about to grab the impressionable kid by the collar and advise him to stay far, far away from her ex if he hoped for an ethical reputation in journalism. But she shouldn't get into anything with Leo. She had no idea about his loyalties or what he was going to write. If he reported on *her* and it was negative, Garry would pitch a fit. He might even fire her for spite.

The more she thought about the whole setup, it felt like *she* was there to audit Jeff, and Leo was there to audit *her*. How could it get any worse?

"Off the record," Leo said. "Is this Cruz guy as nuts as

he seems?"

"No," she snapped. "And that's *on* the record."

Leo chuckled. "What kind of drink did he slip you back there?" He laughed and walked off, jotting in his notebook.

Man, she was a sap. Now that she knew about his connection to Garry, she shouldn't be talking to Leo at all... on or off the record. She should finish her unbiased audit, email the report to Garry before she got canned, then return to real life, forgetting all about Jeff Cruz...and the way he made her open up like a flower.

She caught Jeff's eye, and he gave her a flash of that Han Solo grin. Yeah, forgetting about him would be easier said than done.

A few minutes later, he broke from the group and strolled over. "Okay?"

"Stop asking that," she said through her teeth. "I'm fine, thanks for your help."

"I would say 'ask me again anytime,' but that's probably not a good idea."

"Probably not." She couldn't help laughing. "Um, so Leo mentioned you're using new technology today. I'd like to hear about that when you have a...a few minutes."

They held eye contact for a long moment, and Sharona wondered if—like her—Jeff was thinking about the last time they'd shared a few minutes alone.

"How does Leo know about that?" he finally asked. And why did it look like he was grinding his teeth?

"I'm not sure. But if I were you, I wouldn't share anything important with him."

"Who should I share with?" he asked, tilting his head. "You?"

"Hey, it was just some friendly advice."

"Well, thanks for that. Listen, things are about to get crazy." He slid on a pair of sunglasses. "So I'll be tied up. To be on the safe side, if someone tells you to step back, listen to them—for everyone's safety."

"I won't be in the way," she said, a bit annoyed. It wasn't like she was a natural klutz—seasickness wasn't her fault, and everyone has spilled a drink at least once in their lives—okay, twice, but whatever.

The moment Jeff left, she pulled out her phone about to do a Google search. Maybe if she looked up his name, there would be a clue about the new gadget he was using. There was a new text. From Garry. Instead of texting back, she stepped into the empty helm and gave him a call.

"Sharona," her boss—her ex-fiancé—barked after one ring. "What have you found?"

Not for the first time in her experience of working with him, she got the impression he expected her to dig up something sinister...bust the big, bad scientists for doing deeds unethical.

"Everything checks out," she said. "It's all routine."

"Jobs like this are never routine—that's rule number one." She always hated when he spoke to her like she was an idiot. She didn't appreciate it when they'd been engaged, and she didn't now. If she hadn't really believed in her job—helping small research teams manage their funds more economically—she would not have continued to work with him.

"I guess...they're using some kind of innovative tracking system," she offered. "It's not on the audit list."

There was a pause, then, "Sharona. Listen very carefully:

find out everything you can."

"That's not my job. I didn't come here to spy on…" She cut herself off, took a breath, then glanced toward Leo.

Spy…

"Garry, did you send a reporter from UM?"

She heard the shuffle of papers on his end. "Reporter? No."

She didn't believe him, of course. Leo had already confessed.

"Look, just do your job and report back. UM is paying us a lot of money to do this job."

She rolled her eyes, ready to hang up on him when one of the deckhands called out, "There's the first!"

"Look, Garry, I gotta go—"

"Find out about that tracker, Sharona, or don't bother coming back."

"Yes, sir," she muttered under her breath. She ended the call, then moved to the side of the ship where the same deckhand was pointing out to sea. How these guys had such good eyesight, she'd never know.

"Got it on radar," Pax confirmed.

Jeff wheeled around to them "Break surface?"

The deckhand looked through a pair of binoculars, scanning the water. "Once, but I lost him."

"Damn," Jeff muttered, then turned to Pax. "Anything?"

"Still got him. He's gone deep but within the perimeter." Pax looked at his boss. "Chum?"

Jeff rubbed his chin. "No blood in the water unless it's necessary. Keep an eye on it."

Sharona glanced at Pax's screen, which displayed a radar system, different from the one she'd seen earlier. "Which program is this?" she asked.

Pax just grunted, keeping his eyes on the screen.

"What is the name for auditing purposes?"

He muttered under his breath, then rattled off the name. Sharona found it, typed in a note, then checked it off. Jeez, was that so hard?

She glanced at his screen again. There were a handful of blinking dots she assumed were the sharks. A little ball of dread rolled in her stomach. Not nausea like before—that had been mortifying. And not fear that a great white was going to eat the boat. Her dread was the thought of finally seeing one of the tracking devices Jeff had described. She wasn't in the mood to witness a bunch of blood if Jeff and his team planned on tagging more specimens.

"He's coming up," Pax exclaimed in an excited voice. "Fast."

"Get the trigger ready," Jeff instructed. "Everyone, keep your eyes peeled. Neon pink, remember? Should stand out once it's released. There!"

This time, Sharona easily spotted the dorsal fin.

"*Now!*" Jeff shouted.

A second later, like the cork popping out of a bottle of champagne, a bright pink object the size of a magic marker shot skyward. By the time it landed, the dorsal fin was out of sight.

"All eyes," Jeff said, then he called to the guy posted way up in the eagles nest. "Bogie, you got it?"

The guy held binoculars to his eyes. "Got it in sight, Cruz. To the port, fifteen meters, bobbin' like a damn cork."

"Unbelievable. Spur, Clancy, get the boat and walkies. Mates, this is it…let's get our baby."

Just as Jeff predicted, it got crazy. Sharona stood back, watching in awe at their speed and efficiency. Like a well-oiled machine, everyone knew what to do without being asked, and before she knew it, Jeff and two members of the crew were stepping off the back of the ship and onto a speedboat.

"Where are they going?" she asked Pax, who sat at the bolted-down chair and table in front of his laptop.

"To pick up Old Faithful number nine," he replied.

She scanned her list, already knowing she wouldn't find it. "And that is…?"

He eyed her skeptically for a moment, then sighed. "I guess it's okay to tell you since you're here. The Old Faithful program is detachable trackers. They store data but are too small to transmit tangible intel to the satellites like the large ones everyone uses. If we get close enough when the animal surfaces, we can detach ours remotely."

"And it shoots into the sky," she said, gazing toward the water. "Old Faithful, like the geyser at Yellowstone Park. Cool."

"Cool?" Pax chuckled. "It's more than cool, it's ingenious. Cruz's brain child."

"Huh," she said as she flipped to the front of her list, still not seeing anything called Old Faithful. "Could it be called something else? I don't see that name."

"You won't find it on any inventory list from UM," Pax said. "Jeff funded it out of his own pocket."

She lowered her tablet. "Why?"

"For one thing, other groups have tried using similar prototypes and they've all failed, pretty publically. Jeff was able to partner with a group of engineers in Japan who came up with something radical. He didn't want to get in the news if it didn't work, didn't need cameras from Animal Planet documenting everything."

"I see," Sharona said, and couldn't help feeling impressed. "So now they've gone out to fish this tracker out of the water, so to speak?"

"We counted eight of our Old Faithful-tagged animals in this area. If we're lucky, we'll get all eight trackers today. The intel retrieved will be beyond innovative. This is a scientific first in the field of shark research…if it works the way Jeff hopes."

Sharona nodded, then stepped to the side, watching the smaller boat speed a good twenty meters away. She could see Jeff, his blue shirt and dark hair, now partially covered with a sun visor that was somehow extremely sexy on him. Their boat slowed, made a sharp turn, then Jeff lowered a net attached to a long metal stick over the side.

Complete silence fell over the crew of the *Mad Hatter*, as everyone simultaneously held their breath, waiting. A few seconds later, Jeff straightened and held something high over his head. It was neon pink.

Everyone broke into cheers. Even Manny blew the horn. High fives were given all around, and then the crew raced to the rear of the boat awaiting the return of their leader.

Jeff was grinning wider that she'd ever seen him. He looked exhilarated and ocean-sprayed and just plain gorgeous. Sharona had the flash of an image of him coming out of a shower. What she would do for him to smile at her that way.

"Can you read the data right now? Here?" she asked Pax, keeping an eye on the pink tracker.

"That's the major downfall. These transmitters don't have a USB connection attached organically; that makes them too intrusive while attached to the animal. We'll have to wait until we're back at the lab."

"Hmm," she said, tapping that into her tablet.

"Every time the dorsal fin breaks surface with our tracker attached, it sends a ping to us. In the last year, our sharks have been traced all the way to South Africa and Hawaii. This species has never been tracked so specifically before. Our findings have been astounding."

"How are they attached?" she asked. "Jeff said something about a…a hole-punch."

"Those are for the long-term transmitters. They need to be able to endure up to five years in the water. Cruz refuses to use those now, not with *our* system. The Old Faithfuls are short-term, meant to stay attached for two years at the most so we can map their migration. For attaching purposes, in layman's terms, we use a waterproof Velcro."

"And they detach electronically?"

Pax nodded. "Completely battery operated. The whole thing flies off, barely leaving a mark on the fin."

After recording all that in the notes section of her database, she said, "Thank you. I appreciate this information. When I talked to Jeff about the trackers earlier, he didn't say anything about this. I think he's a little protective."

Pax laughed darkly and squinted into the sun. "Yeah, well, you would be, too, if you'd been trying to get approval for five years. Before that, even, he'd been nearly ready to patent an early prototype of Old Faithful when it was stolen."

"By who? A competitor?"

"No." Pax shifted in his seat like he'd divulged something

he shouldn't have.

What were they hiding?

"Let's just say, a lot of the other teams don't worry about getting consent through the proper channels," Pax added. "But Cruz never skips a step. Our team is different."

"How so?"

"You won't find excessive amounts of chum aboard this ship, and very little bait. We do our best to not disturb the ecosystem whenever possible. We study their behavior so we can go to them instead of forcing them to come to us by pouring gallons of blood into the ocean. That was Jeff's idea, too, and that philosophy in itself is innovative."

"Sounds like you guys are pretty protective of these animals."

Pax shook his head, his expression closing up. "I shouldn't have said anything," he muttered. "You're a conservationist, aren't you?"

Sharona blinked. It sounded like an insult. "I'm an animal lover, yes. But I'm not here to judge what you're doing—my job is to collect facts."

"Here's this for a fact: you probably think you're the one campaigning for more humane treatment of these animals," Pax said, staring her dead in the eyes. "But all you're doing is getting in the way."

She didn't know how to reply to that, because she didn't know if it was the truth. Was SED Auditors—or more specifically—was *she* in Jeff's way?

Pax gathered his laptop. "No wonder Cruz was as pissed off as I'd ever seen him the second you stepped aboard this vessel." He shook his head, then walked away.

She stared after him, feeling a knot in her stomach. Was

Jeff really that strongly against her being here? Was that kiss just what he'd claimed it was? Maybe he didn't want to have to deal with the paperwork of someone being injured while aboard the ship, or he'd done whatever he could to keep from turning back to the mainland and scrapping the whole day.

She felt hurt and deflated at the thought.

Once back aboard the *Mad Hatter*, Jeff was accepting high fives from everyone. But there wasn't much time for congratulations, because only a few minutes later, Pax announced another tracker had broken surface less than a mile away. And they were off.

In the next few hours, Sharona met with different members of the crew and managed to get through most of the auditing list. There were only a few minor discrepancies, and she couldn't account for a two thousand dollar deposit on one of the pressure pumps. Other than that, everything was, for lack of a better term…shipshape.

While she worked, three more transmitters were retrieved. She watched Jeff go out on the speedboat to grab the device. She tried her best to stay completely out of his way, to do her job and only observe the crew celebrate every time one of those hot-pink corks shot into the air.

Jeff's obvious nonexistence wherever she happened to be standing was duly noted, and after a while, Sharona was ready to get off the boat. No reason to be where she wasn't wanted. She'd just finished wolfing down a sandwich and was chatting with Manny when a sixth device was spotted.

"Thirty meters south," Pax reported. "This might be the last we get today. I'll go out for it."

"I've got it," Jeff said, breezing by where she sat on the

leaning post. "Grab some tucker and shade, mate."

"Sure you don't need a break?" Pax asked.

Jeff squinted out at the blue, rippling ocean. "Bogie's driving the boat, water's calm as glass, no need for three. Unless…" He glanced at Sharona. "Why don't you come out?"

It was the first time he'd spoken to her in hours. "Are you sure? Don't want to be in your way." She cringed at the bitter, immature tone in her voice.

Jeff looked at her. "I wouldn't suggest it if I thought you'd be in the way." His tone matched hers. "But if you're not up to it, no worries. I just thought you'd like a different perspective than what you see on your list there. More to report back."

Well, this was true, and it wasn't as if the speedboat was an inflatable raft. It was bigger than her car at home. And so what if Jeff was all business? Hadn't he said that was the way it had to be, anyway? And like an idiot, hadn't she agreed?

"Okay," she said.

Jeff cocked his head. "Ladies first."

Chapter Six

"Look, I know you don't want me here," Sharona said under her breath as she walked beside Jeff toward the chase boat.

He caught the hostile tone in her voice. What had changed in the past three hours? They'd discussed it and hadn't they both agreed they were there to do their jobs?

Sheilas... Who the hell knows what they're thinking? He couldn't figure *this* one out at all, and he wasn't sure he should want to so badly.

His mind replayed the other time he'd allowed his business life to mix with his private life. That fatal slipup had cost him a year of research, and set the Old Faithful project way behind schedule because his early data had been pinched from right under his nose.

How could he have known the woman he'd trusted with his whole heart enough to marry could have betrayed him like that?

"You're pissed that I'm here," Sharona said. "I get that,

and I've been trying to stay out of your way—as much as humanly possible given the circumstances. Just remember, *you're* the one who invited me to retrieve the transmitter. And you're the one who...you know...in the helm. So don't go saying I muscled my way in."

Jeff stared at her, feeling even more baffled. Though he did enjoy that her feisty, sharklike attitude was back. After she huffed and turned away, he shook his head and stepped onto the speedboat. Despite those long legs, it was a bit of a jump for her, so he reached out a hand. She glared at it, acting stubborn.

"Give me your damn hand, Sharona, unless you're hankering for a dip."

"Fine," she muttered.

Once he had ahold of her, he gave her arm a tug. She stumbled on her landing, crashing into his chest. He caught her easily, not unhappy about the misstep bringing her body straight into his arms.

"Luckily you didn't have a drink in your hand," he said. Sharona exhaled a little laugh. "You can sit." He pointed to the bench seat attached to the back of the small helm. "Or stand," he added, gesturing to the spot next to him, trying not to be overly pleased when she took that spot beside him, taking a firm hold on the railing. Bogie didn't drive very fast, and the floor of the boat was deep enough that only the wave of a breeching humpback would knock her around on a calm day like today.

Once they were both in place, Bogie pulled away from the mother ship.

Jeff had the walkie to his ear, relaying Pax's direction toward the floating transmitter out in the open ocean. With their course locked in, he turned his attention to Sharona, taking in her long dark hair blowing in the breeze. She was holding it back in a ponytail with one hand, exposing her long neck. Why hadn't he kissed her there? Suddenly, it was all he could think about.

"How far are we going?" she asked, breaking his concentration.

"The, uh, the tracker drifted a bit," he said, pulling his eyes from the mesmerizing contours of her throat. "Maybe a hundred meters. Might have to circle a while."

She nodded. He didn't like how detached she seemed. Maybe he'd sent a mixed message when he'd kissed her. Although, he didn't know what the hell kind of message he'd meant to send.

Even if what he felt for her was the start of something real, how could they make it work past today's job? There was no way he could move to...where did she say she was from? Hershey?

Yeah, not many great whites in central Pennsylvania, Cruz.

"What do sharks find so special about this area off the coastline?" she said. "I mean, if you don't *mind* my asking."

That icy tone was back. Jeff didn't like it. "I don't mind. Whenever you have questions, just ask."

She nodded but seemed as skeptical as before.

"A lot of our tagged sharks are here, though we don't know why yet. Our research takes longer because it's less aggressive."

She glanced at him, biting her lip, looking pensive.

"What?"

"Nothing." She exhaled. "It's just...this whole thing is a

lot more humane than what I imagined."

"We're not here to hurt any wildlife on or offshore."

She nodded. "I can see that."

After a moment of trying to read that look in her eyes, Jeff gave up and laughed. "I hate to think what you expected to discover today. I mean, aside from me poaching money from the uni to fund my personal booze cruise."

Sharona laughed. He liked the sound of it, reminding him of how she'd giggled and tossed her hair last night. "I never once thought that." She tucked some hair behind an ear, trying to keep it from blowing in her face. Jeff's fingers twitched, wishing he could hold it back for her. "In my line of work, I've learned to expect the worst."

"You've come across that many crooks?"

"You'd be surprised. I was originally hired as an intern while in grad school finishing my accounting degree. I always got the feeling I was being given the...*special* cases. Like I could make people tell me things they shouldn't. I still feel that way."

It was pretty easy to picture this. About ten seconds into their first kiss, if she'd asked him, he would've gladly divulged all of his ATM codes and the combination to his gun safe and his grandmum's Tax File Number. Though he was sure Sharona Blaire wasn't sent to make out with every auditing assignment. The thought actually made him want to laugh.

"What do you mean by special cases?" he asked.

"Like I'm supposed to *find* something," she explained. "Sometimes I do, but I can always tell when it's one of those cases."

"And you felt that about today?"

"Sort of. But thanks to Pax and some of the other guys,

the audit's almost done. Everything is pretty much perfect."

"Well, that's a relief. I must be better at hiding my crimes than I thought." He leaned toward her. "Joking."

She exhaled a quiet laugh and looked down at the water. Sunlight bounced off the surface, sending bursts of sunny brightness across her face.

"Aside from all that, though," she said, "and on a personal note, I've been really impressed with how you run your team. Obviously my job doesn't have to do with marine life, but I've audited research teams similar to yours and you can't believe the crap I've seen people try to get away with—really dangerous, irresponsible things. Damaging. I've always been a believer that science, too, needs its checks and balances. But even as an auditor, I also believe both sides should come together to make the planet a better place."

"Isn't that what you and I have been doing?"

When she finally lifted a genuine smile, Jeff hadn't realized how much he'd missed it. "Exactly like what we've been doing," she said. "I'm not in your way and you're not in mine. In the grand scheme of things, we share a mutual goal, but I'm not a distraction."

He couldn't help laughing, probably loudly enough to scare a school of hammerheads.

"What?"

"Sharona Blaire." He shook his head, keeping his eyes on the smooth ocean surface. "You've been nothing but the sexiest, most desirable distraction of my life." The admission hung in the air, suspended, and for a painful moment, he regretted being so open...trusting.

"I guess that means we have something else in common, Jeff Cruz."

Sharona didn't know if she should say more or simply wrestle Jeff to the floor of the boat.

Jumping to conclusions was the very thing she had to fight against whenever she went on a job. She dealt in facts and numbers, nothing else. And here she'd been assuming what Pax had told her about Jeff being personally pissed at her was the truth…without bothering to ask Jeff about it.

It might've been the biggest relief in her life when he'd called her sexy, like it was a fact. Though the situation wasn't ideal by any stretch, neither of them could ignore their combustible chemistry.

"We're nearly there." His words snapped her awake.

"Great," she said, wiping her sweaty palms over her shorts. "So, why *do* you think this area is popular with your sharks?" she asked again, needing to fill her thoughts with something besides how she felt the involuntarily urge to lick her lips whenever she looked at Jeff.

"Like I mentioned before, we suspect it's a place they come to mate." He shifted his weight and pressed his shoulder against hers, their bare arms touching. "But there isn't much information yet."

"What about the data on Old Faithful?"

"Did Pax explain the Old Faithful project?"

"It wasn't on my list and I was curious."

He lifted an eyebrow and leaned against the side of the boat. "Afraid I was one of your special cases?"

She laughed. "Maybe. What he told me, though, it's fascinating. I'd love to know more."

"When we're back on the ship, I'll walk through the whole process with you."

"That'd be great." She smiled and turned toward the water. "So, will the data give you any indication of why the sharks come here?"

He shook his head. "Doubtful. White sharks are quite elusive when it comes to reproduction."

"Interesting. In what way?"

"Well, there are very few documented cases of anyone witnessing white sharks in the act."

"Of mating?"

He nodded. It made Sharona want to laugh, how serious he looked. "Obviously, though, we know it happens, since the species isn't extinct. Plus, there are telltale signs."

"Like what?"

"Tangible evidence of intense force. Scars on their dermal denticles scales, tears, cuts, gashes from teeth." He tipped his chin forward, bending his face to hers. "Though I'd rather think of them as love bites." His gaze flicked to her mouth then away.

A sizzle broke out on the back of her neck, and the part of her arm touching Jeff felt like it was on fire. "Love bites," she echoed in a whisper.

He nodded. "There's documented proof that mature sharks who've mated are left with very specific markings."

"Like it's...rough?" she asked, feeling her heart pound, throat go dry.

"*Passionate*," he tweaked, pressing his shoulder against hers again. She knew it was a deliberate move this time. "Or maybe it's the way the male grips her and holds on...the most intense lover's embrace in the animal kingdom. With creatures that have teeth sharper than knives, obviously that kind of shagging leaves very impressive dents. When it comes down to it…in the throes of passion, our species aren't so different. I know I've learned a lot from my personal research."

"Love bites…" she repeated, her voice coming out as a whisper. "Fascinating."

"It is." He matched her slow, hushed tone. "I shouldn't brag, but I'm one of the top experts in my field."

She swallowed. "Of shark sex, you mean."

"Well, that, too. Anything you want to know on the subject, Sharona…anything"—he pulled back a sexy half grin—"I'd be happy to enlighten you."

Chapter Seven

Jeff loved the way Sharona's cheeks became more and more flushed. He'd never seen anything more beautiful than her on a boat in the middle of the ocean. Though he could picture her in a few other places he'd like to compare.

"I see it!" She wore an excited grin, her brown eyes bright. A few feet to the left, floating like a piece of driftwood, was gorgeous Old Faithful number five, the one worn by their old mate, Waltzing Matilda.

"Should I grab the net?" Sharona asked. She must have been paying attention to the other retrieval trips because she already had the long pole in her hand, the dripping net off the side.

"Bogie will come about," Jeff said. "Then pass the net to me. Or, why don't you do the honors. Bogie, get us right up along side."

The boat slowly came about, so the tag would be within easy reach.

"Ready?" he said to Sharona, who looked as excited as a little girl seeing her first joey. Quite different from the woman who'd almost lost her tucker a few hours ago.

"I'm ready," she said, grinning and gripping the pole.

"We're slowing. Wait till we come to a complete stop, though. No need to fish you out, too. Although, isn't it time for *you* to be the one in the wet shirt?"

She eyed him over her shoulder and giggled. "Will you ever let me live that down?"

"I don't plan on it," he said with a grin as Bogie cut the engine, allowing the boat to drift. The hot-pink transmitter was only a few feet away.

"I think I can reach it."

"Make sure you've got a good grip and your feet are stable."

She rose up on her toes a few times. "Stable, sir."

"Go for it."

She pressed the front of her hips against the boat and bent over the side, far enough to dip the net into the water, giving Jeff a mighty sweet view. As she was about to scoop up the transmitter, he heard shouts coming from the mother ship and Pax's voice crackled through the walkie.

"Pull back! Matilda."

Ice shot up Jeff's spine as he watched Sharona teetering over the edge of the boat.

"I got it!" she said triumphantly. Before she could lift the net out of the water, he spotted the fin, then the nose of Matilda. In about two seconds, the shark would be on top of them.

He lunged Sharona's way. "Arm inside!"

She gawked at him. "Wha—"

There was a huge splash, drenching him, then multiple splashes.

Before he could make another move, the entire net, as well as its contents, were ripped away by the shark's jaws. Jeff had a tight hold of Sharona and yanked her back. She shrieked, still clutching the gnarled pole. One single bite and Matilda has chomped clean through the metal.

"Drop it," Jeff said. When she did, he saw the blood.

Sharona was *not* going to lose control of her stomach again. Not for the second time in one day. What would everyone think? If news got back, Garry would give her milquetoast assignments the rest of her career.

She *had* to hold it together, though her churning stomach from hanging upside down over the side of the boat, then being yanked back made that pretty difficult.

"You're hurt," Jeff said, one of his arms clamping tightly around her. His sexy accent was like music to her ears, already soothing her ails. "Where did she get you?"

She looked at him, trying to appear steady and calm and not about to puke on his shoes. "Who?"

"You're bit—she breeched so fast. Damn it—I didn't even see her get you."

His rapid-fire words, the pale, frantic look on his face… Confusion filled Sharona's chest with the cold burn of panic.

"Bit? I don't…" That's when she noticed the blood. Before jumping to the most terrifying conclusion, she noted that all her fingers were intact and also that the pole she'd been holding, the one that was halfway gone now; the other half either in the stomach of a shark or on its way to Davy Jones's Locker.

"It's a cut." She'd never had a weak stomach about blood, though it wasn't exactly jolly seeing her own all over the white floor of the speedboat.

"Where?" Jeff gently took her wrist to look at her hand. "Too jagged for a shark bite," he noted, examining her palm, sounding confused but relieved.

"It's from the pole. I was trying to keep a grip on it when…." She had a sudden flash of the white underside, the black eye, rows of teeth. *Oy.*

Maybe thinking she was about to sway back, Jeff took her around the waist. "You're okay," he whispered. "It's not a bad cut. I've had worse, I promise." He pulled her to his chest, one hand rubbing her back.

She didn't fight it; her hand did sting…a little bit. Besides, it felt really nice to have someone taking care of her for a change. With four younger siblings and an ex-fiancé who'd never learned to do his own laundry, she'd done most of the protecting and caretaking throughout her life. So she rested a cheek against Jeff's firm chest, breathing in the smell of his shirt—now wet from the ocean—and listened to his words of comfort. She felt his heart beating, faster than hers.

"It's not that bad—"

He shushed her, called for Bogie to get the first-aid kit, then pulled her to the bench seat and eased her down.

"Let me see it again."

Sharona opened her clenched fist, displaying her gashed palm. "It stings more than anything," she said as salt water trickled into the center.

"Doesn't look deep." He placed a cotton pad in the

middle of her palm over the cut. "Hold this on there until we get back to the ship, then we'll treat it. Let's go, Bogie."

Sharona stared down at the mangled pole on the floor, reality hitting. *Oh, no. What did I do?* She swallowed hard, then peered up at Jeff, at his earnest blue eyes fixed on her. "I'm so sorry, Jeff," she said, sudden tears stinging her eyes. "I can't believe I did that."

"Did what? You could've lost an arm. They don't usually get that close." His grip around her tightened. "I don't know what I was thinking, letting you hang halfway over the bloody side."

"I mean about the transmitter. I dropped it. Or…the shark ate it."

He examined her hand again, then placed it on his thigh. "Accidents happen. All that matters is you're safe." He ran his hand down her arm, shoulder to fingertips. "You might need this again."

He was being so sweet, even after she'd totally screwed up. Every time he touched her or stroked her skin reassuringly, her stomach cartwheeled. She wanted to thank him properly. To touch his face, run her fingers through his hair. Then she wanted to straddle his lap and show him how she truly felt. But before long, they pulled up to the stern of the *Mad Hatter*.

She felt a little embarrassed as the crew gawked in silence. Despite all the blood—there goes another shirt— it was just a cut. She totally loved the attention from Jeff, though, and missed the safe feeling of his arms being around her. Maybe she should've played out the panic a little longer while they were alone. Who knew if she would ever get the chance again.

"Nothing to see here," Sharona called out to the crew. "Just a classic klutz with a weak stomach. And it's only a Bloody Mary cocktail."

Jeff burst into laughter and pulled her in so his chin rested on top of her head. "You make me laugh," he whispered. A second later, he let go so they could stand. "She's all right, guys," he added as he helped her step onto the ship. "The *pole* bit her, not Matilda. Though I do suspect our girl down there has a bit of a crush."

"Lucky me," Sharona said.

Some of the guys laughed politely, and Jeff slid an arm around her shoulders. "We do need to get this washed. I'll take her below."

He pulled her tight to his side as they walked toward the companionway, Sharona holding her hurt hand against her chest as they went. He let her go down the ladder first but stayed right behind her. "There," he said, pointing to the rear of the quarters. "Have a seat on my bunk."

The tiny dozen or so individual sleeping areas were cut into the hull of the ship, like little caves, only big enough for a bed and a few shelves for clothes and personal items. She sat on the bunk and bounced a few times. It had a nice spring to it.

"Before I get the first aid kit," Jeff said, "let me grab something dry—I'm soaked. And looks like you've got a spot or two on you." He eyed the front of her shirt. Though the spilled tomato juice had been a cheerier shade of red, the blood from her cut certainly did the job. He leaned toward where she sat on the bunk and reached behind her to retrieve two T-shirts from the duffel bag on his shelf. "Will be a little large on you, I'm afraid," he said, handing her one.

"Thank you."

They stared at each other for a few still, silent moments… an unspoken standoff of Who-Will-Take-Off-Their-Shirt-First.

Jeff cleared his throat, then dropped his gaze, making a point of looking out the small, round window. Sharona quickly peeled off her blood-splattered top, feeling irrationally shy. Jeff's replacement T-shirt swam on her, the neck hole sliding off both shoulders, but at least it was clean and dry, and had a faint whiff of its sexy owner.

In the two seconds it took to get herself situated, Jeff had pulled his shirt over his head. She couldn't help staring at his perfect chest, the tan lines and flat muscles. The sensitive nerves at the tips of her fingers twitched, longing to touch him, trace along the smooth skin. As he turned to the side to toss his wet shirt over a chair, her breath caught.

"Jeff! What is that?" She couldn't pull her eyes away from the long, shiny imprints running in a half circle from the top of his shoulder to the middle of his side, crossing over his spine.

He took a step back and angled that side of his body away. "It's just a scar."

"From what?" Without thinking, she stretched out a hand and ran the back of her finger over the jagged lines, dozens of tiny triangles…the exact size of—

"Shark," he said softly. "I was sixteen."

"This is from one bite?" Her heart beats came slower and heavier while her throat began to close, making it hard to breathe. "It's…it's half your body."

"She was a great white, seventeen, eighteen footer," Jeff said, his voice hushed but steady. "Or so my surfing mates told me. I never saw the whole thing. Just the face. The eye."

"Jeff," she whispered, her hand skimming across the part of the scar over his stomach. "Can you tell me what happened?"

He nodded slowly but didn't speak right away, staring past her shoulder at nothing. "We…we knew we shouldn't have been out there," he finally began. "There'd been sightings all day, but"—he paused to shrug—"we wanted to catch some waves. We weren't thinking. Anyway, I was about to take the next curl when something knocked my board. I saw a shadow but didn't piece it together fast enough. Wouldn't have mattered anyway, there was nothing I could do. When she knocked me again, I wiped out. I was disoriented in the water, tossing in the waves when I felt another bump. That's when she had me."

"*Had* you?"

Silently, he drew a half circle across his stomach, following the scar. "Funny thing is, she had my arm inside her mouth but it didn't have a scratch on it after."

"How did you get away?" Sharona asked through her tightening throat.

"She didn't want to eat me. I'd pissed her off, being in her territory. She shook me around for a while, but I was lucky she never rolled me down; instead she kept us on the surface so I could breathe. I kept digging my fingers into her eye until she got tired and let go."

Sharona's mouth fell open but all she could do was shake her head, wordlessly.

"I lost a lot of blood, but like I said, she wasn't trying to kill me. Sharks are territorial and I was on her turf. In a way, it was my fault."

"But…you study sharks now," she said. "After you were attacked, I'd think you would hate them."

"Hate?" he repeated, tipping his chin to gaze down at her. "They're fascinating. I became obsessed with studying them, figuring out how they think and why they behave the way they do. We share a planet with them. I have a healthy fear, but hate?" He shook his head. "It's the closest thing to true love."

She stared at him, taking in his words. "What you said last night," she whispered. "About not taking your shirt off in front of just anyone." She touched a finger to the scar, feeling the warmth of his skin, his beautiful soul beneath. "Is this why?"

"It freaks people out," he answered in a strangled voice that made her ache to hold him, comfort him.

"Jeff…" She rose to her feet and stood before him, running a hand up his stomach, feeling the flat planes. When she reached the top of the scar, she pressed both palms flat against him, moving up along his smooth skin. She felt his hard muscles flex when she reached the notch at the center of his chest. She splayed her fingers, needing to explore more, but suddenly, he caught her wrists.

"We…" He started, then swallowed, glancing away. "We need to tend to your cut." He let go and disappeared around a corner.

Sharona exhaled and slumped back onto the bunk, trying to catch her breath. Jeff returned carrying a larger first-aid kit than what had been on the speedboat. He was still shirtless, the dry one draped over his shoulder. The bunk she was on wasn't big and when he sat beside her, she could smell the salty tang of the sea mixed with something clean

$\mathcal{L}$OVE $\mathcal{B}$ITES

and manly. Her desire was almost blinding.

He took her hand and poured antiseptic into the hollow of the palm. It stung worse than the salt water.

"If it hurts, that means it's working," he said, probably noticing her flinch. But there was a smile in his voice. He pulled her hand toward him and rested it on his thigh. "So, are you ever going to tell me what happened?" he asked, looking down at her hand as he continued to clean the wound.

"I told you, it was the pole, I was trying—"

"I meant last night." He lifted his eyes to her. "Sharona, why didn't you come back to me?"

Chapter Eight

When she didn't reply, Jeff lowered his eyes, running a finger across her palm. The cut wasn't bad, and he knew he didn't need to coddle her. But the way she'd been staring at his scar... It had shaken her up, as it did with other women.

But Sharona wasn't like other women. It wasn't horror in her eyes as he expected, or even pity. She seemed touched... in a loving way. She was brave and caring and feisty, like the sharks he loved, though more of a beaut than even the most stunning great whites. It sucked that they'd lost Matilda's tracker, but that was nothing compared to what could have happened.

If she hadn't been injured—as minor as it was—Jeff might have manned up and finally finished that kiss, the one that had started at the hotel pub yet felt incomplete all these hours later.

Why the hell had he killed the mood by bringing up last night?

$\mathcal{L}$OVE $\mathcal{B}$ITES

"Oh," she said, lifting her eyes to his. "You noticed that, did you?"

"I'm a scientist. It's my job to catch the details. And yes, I did notice your acute absence. And I didn't like it."

"Sorry." She dropped her gaze to the floor.

"I don't want an apology, Sharona. I want to know what happened. If you changed your mind, I get it." He paused and ran a hand over his face. "You were the one who started it."

"I know." She lifted her chin. "I've never done anything like that—come on to a stranger. Never even instigated a kiss before." She laughed, but it was dark and self-conscious—not like the woman he was getting to know. "I guess I was giving myself permission because I was in a foreign country for one night."

He leaned away from her instinctively. "So I was an experiment?"

"No. I thought it might be…an adventure." She lowered her gaze again. "I was into it, into *you*. Which I'm sure you knew."

"I had a pretty good idea," he said, relieved that he hadn't imagined it.

"I know it's silly, but before we went to your room, I wanted to brush my teeth. I'd been traveling all day and felt a little worn out." She smiled. "I didn't want to feel worn out with you."

"That's why you went to your room?"

She nodded. "When I got there and had two seconds to think without you kissing me and making my brain mush, I realized I couldn't go through with it. I'm not a one-night-stand kind of girl, Jeff. I'm sorry I gave you that impression."

She fidgeted with her rings; it was her nervous habit he'd noticed. "I was trying to be someone different for a change. But at the heart of me, I'm not that person."

When she finally paused to breathe, Jeff blew out a long, relieved exhale followed by a laugh that shook the bunk.

"What?" she asked, sounding a little hurt.

He scrubbed at his jaw. "Sharona, I'm not that person, either. It was shocking how it happened, but before I knew it, I was too caught up. Of course I was attracted to you, but I knew there was nothing I could do about it, not with me leaving the next morning. I'm not built that way."

"That's surprising."

"My mother taught us manners."

"Remind me to thank her."

He tried to ignore the way her smile made the pit of his stomach fill with heat and burn with lightning, another wave of want pulling him toward this woman. "There were five of us boys," he added.

"I have four siblings, too."

He touched a lock of her hair. "I know. You told me about your family last night. It's funny, I didn't know your name, but I knew about your childhood and your first boyfriend and how you failed your driving test. It was like we'd gone on five dates in two hours."

"I felt the same way, like we were friends as kids and were playing catch-up."

He glanced down, adjusting the gauze around her hand. "What was it like growing up in the chocolate capitol of the world?"

"What?" Her forehead furrowed at the question. "Oh. No, *Natalie's* from Hershey. We met in college. I grew up in

Tampa."

Jeff took a few beats before asking, "Is that where you live now?"

No, he couldn't possibly be so lucky. First, meeting an amazing woman like Sharona one night, then remeeting her the next day. But this?

She shook her head. "My parents are still there, but I moved to Miami for school and fell in love with it."

Jeff sat back—this was beyond amazing. "*I* live in Miami, too."

They were quiet for a moment. The only sounds were the chatters from topside. Sounded like everyone above deck was busy preparing the ship for their next stop. Also meaning, no one would be coming down.

"That's…" she said, her dark eyes blinking once, slowly. "Handy."

"I travel a lot for work, obviously. My funding comes from UM, but I work out of the uni, too. It's my home base. And here I assumed our meeting was an accident."

"I don't spill my drinks on just any man, you know." She touched his cheek. "Only dashing shark lovers with panty-dropping accents."

He chuckled and looked down, running a finger over the inside of her wrist. "I was more than willing to let last night progress naturally, even though it wasn't my style, either. I went along with it because…well, you really didn't give me a choice."

"I was that irresistible last night?"

"Last night?" Jeff couldn't help saying. "Try right now. Try every damn second since you stepped aboard this vessel."

Sharona took in a quiet breath, then held it, like Jeff was

holding his, all the while his heart picked up speed, galloping like a mountain brumby.

"I haven't been able to stop thinking about you," he admitted. "Or that kiss. All of them."

"I know. It's like, we aren't done. Like every kiss is…"

"Not enough."

The air between them sparked.

Jeff didn't give her a chance to make the first move like last night. He wanted to take over, take the pressure off them both to be something they weren't.

He slid a hand behind her head and pulled her to him, getting a fresh taste of her lips. She leaned in, resting her hands on his chest, her touch against his bare skin burned into his blood. Right as he was about to pull her closer, she threw her arms around his neck and crushed her soft body against him, knocking his head against the low-hanging arch of the bunk.

"Sorry," she whispered. "Are you all right?"

He didn't speak, but looked her once more in the eyes, touched his forehead to hers, then scooped his hands under her perfect ass, lifted her up, and laid her flat on the bunk.

As soon as her head hit the soft bed, Sharona was on autopilot, reacting on instinct and blinding passion. What her instinct told her, what every fiber in her body *screamed*, was to hold onto Jeff Cruz and not let go.

His body hovered over her, braced by his elbows, while his hot mouth pressed against hers, sweet and firm, pushing her head deeper into the bed. She ran her fingers through his hair, knotting at the back of his head, keeping him close. There was barely enough room on the bunk for one person, let alone two, especially when one was the size of Jeff.

Finally, he lowered on top of her, moving his mouth to her cheek and ear. She dug her fingers into the back of his head, arching as he ran his lips under her jaw, then across her neck. His breath was hot and perfect against her skin and her heart thumped like the engine of a motorboat.

Sensing what she wanted next, he skimmed his hands down her sides, sliding up the inside of her too-big T-shirt. In response, she wrapped her legs around him and clung to his shoulders, feeling hard, toned muscles and smooth bare skin. She needed to be skin to skin with him, needed her stupid clothes out of the way, so she lifted her arms over her head to remove her shirt, but ended up bashing her hands against the bunk like an oaf.

Jeff lifted his chin, his blue eyes like the deep blue of a sea she could swim in forever. "This might not work," he whispered, his breath coming in jagged, desperate pants.

"Give me two seconds and I'll make it work," she promised, attempting to twist so she could pull off the tangled T-shirt if he wasn't going to do it. "Why is this bunk so *tiny*?"

He smiled fiendishly and dipped his chin, planting hot kisses along her collarbone. Sharona forgot all about her clothes when Jeff secured one of her wrists and held it above her head, pinning her in place, his mouth moving slowly up the inside of her arm. With her free hand, she cradled the back of his head and moved to his neck. When her mouth found the spot she liked, she hovered there, breathing in, tasting the salty, manly tang of his skin. Then, with every part of her body that was connected to his—her arm, her legs around him, her mouth on his neck—she clamped down.

Jeff's body jolted over her, and he drew in a hard, sharp breath. She giggled against his neck as she loosened her grip. After one last suck and gentle nibble, she removed her mouth from his neck.

"Were those your teeth?" he asked, pulling back to look at her, a sexy, questioning gleam in his eyes.

"Just a little love bite," she whispered, running the back of a finger across the spot, admiring her work. "I thought you should know how good it's *supposed* to feel." Tenderly, she kissed the fading welt, feeling his body tremble. "I hope I wasn't too rough for you, Mr. Great White."

Jeff gazed down with an expression she couldn't read. "Damn it all, Sharona," he said with a new fire behind his eyes. His mouth was over hers before she was able to take a breath. She parted her lips, wanted to open everything for him like she never had before. She wiggled, trying again to peel off her top. This time, Jeff was there to help.

"Slowly," he whispered. "Allow me." He moved his hand onto her bare stomach, then inched up the hem of his T-shirt she wore, exposing her lacy bra a centimeter at a time. "You should always wear nothing but my clothes." The look of concentration and admiration on his face was killing her.

"You're so beautiful," he said, dipping his chin to kiss her collarbone, the middle of her stomach, the spot right below the front clasp of her bra.

"I want…" she panted, wrapping her legs around him even tighter.

"Shhh. Hold on," he whispered, his lips touching her mouth as he took her wrists again and held them above her head.

Sharona was all good with foreplay, but seriously, a full day of it was enough. When she struggled to pull free, he placed an index finger over her mouth, and she heard footsteps coming down the ladder.

"Cruz?"

Pax, though she couldn't see him.

Jeff sighed against her neck. "Yeah?" he answered while gazing down at her, a beckoning fire blazing behind his eyes.

"We're about ready. Everything is stowed. Manny says another five."

"Yeah, thanks, mate. Be right there."

A second later, she heard movement up the ladder.

"Sorry," Jeff whispered.

"It's better than him walking in thirty seconds later." She nipped his earlobe. "Trust me."

"Damn. And I was just about to show you a more interesting meaning for 'down under.'" His eyes crinkled at the edges. "But I don't pay Pax enough to keep that information from getting back to the crew."

Sharona still had a hold of him. His smell, the smooth, warm skin and muscles were too delicious to let go of. Since Jeff didn't seem in a hurry to roll off, she gave him a squeeze, slid her hands as far down the curve of his back as she could reach, then kissed him.

His response was unlike the other kisses they'd shared. Up until now, they'd been fevered and frantic, fueled by passion and dangerous timing. But now, Jeff took his time, trading breaths and touches and caresses, like he wanted to milk those five minutes until he had to rejoin the crew above. With each tender movement of his mouth and hands,

Sharona felt bits of her brain melt away, her bones turning to liquid, melting into him.

He ran a hand through her hair and kissed every inch of her mouth, her cheeks. This was the longest moment they'd been alone since last night, but still…incomplete. Every touch made her anticipate what would come next.

After one last deep kiss, Jeff slowly exhaled and collapse on top of her, but then quickly rolled to the side, half of his large body hanging off the bunk. "I have to get up there," he said, his sweet, labored breath caressing her ear.

"I know."

"But believe me, I'm not finished with you, baby." He kissed the side of her neck, sending shivers through her bloodstream.

She exhaled a quiet, dreamy moan of pleasure, stroking the back of his head. "Not even close to finished."

He rolled all the way off the bunk and onto his knees, resting his forearms on the bunk and dropping his chin like he was positioned for bedtime prayer. She heard his breath and saw his back raising and falling with each inhale.

She pulled in her knees, swung her legs over the side of the bunk, and sat up. Jeff placed a hand on her knee, running a thumb over her skin, moving it farther up her thigh. When their eyes locked, she lifted an eyebrow.

"I better get out of here," he said. "I think Manny would overcharge me if we destroy this bunk."

"Tease," she said, pinching his ear.

He laughed and rolled onto the balls of his feet, then stood. "It might be awkward," he said, almost like an afterthought. "With our jobs, you know."

"You're worried about that, too?"

"I meant about going topside together. But you mean?"

"After that," she said, with a touch of dread. "Tomorrow. Back in Miami. What do you think?"

He crouched down and took her chin in one hand. "I think it will work. We're on the same side. I realized that today."

"So did I," she said, feeling tears of relief burn her throat.

"Nothing remotely unethical went down," he added. "No confidences were breached and absolutely no favoritism."

Unable to repress the desire, she reached out to cradle his face in her hands. She pressed her lips to his forehead, his cheek, his ear. "No favoritism?" she whispered while nibbling his earlobe.

Jeff snickered. "The last ten minutes do not count." After one more kiss, he said, "I should go up first. I don't worry about Pax or Manny or the other guys." He shook his head. "It's that reporter…"

"He'd have a field day," she agreed.

Sharona hated that they had to part again, with so much unfinished business between them, but she knew it had to be done. A voice inside her whispered that they would get their chance, the real chance they deserved.

Jeff set his intense blue eyes on her one last time. "See you up there," he said, then started up the ladder.

Sharona sprang from the bunk. "Wait!"

He turned back and ran a frustrated hand down his face. "Believe me, baby, I know it sucks. I want you right now, you have no idea what I want to do to—"

"No," she said with a laugh. "*I* don't mind you walking around half-dressed—I actually prefer it, but it might look suspicious to the others." She tossed him his T-shirt that had somehow gotten wedged under her back.

Jeff chuckled and turned an adorable shade of pink. "Oh yes, um, thanks." Much to her disappointment, he pulled the shirt over his head, covering up that magnificent chest. Even his scar was beautiful—it explained so much about who Jeff was, what he'd been through, was fighting for...the man she was falling headfirst for.

As she watched him climb the ladder, Sharona realized how obvious it was that she hadn't been in love with Garry—not the way she should have been. How she felt about Jeff—the admiration, the pure chemistry—was so much stronger, more real somehow. She didn't just want him, she needed him. Even the illogical aspects of their future seemed... logical. Despite how she'd been down on love only a day ago, now, she couldn't help feeling optimistic.

Chapter Nine

Jeff hoped he looked more composed than he felt when he walked onto the deck. Everyone was busy doing their jobs and Manny was the only one who gave him a second look. Well, he gave the still-tingling location on Jeff's neck a second look. Jeff chose not to react.

"Shoving off?" he asked the captain while tucking in his shirt. Had his other been tucked in before his little tumble with Sharona? He couldn't remember.

"Just about to," Manny replied. "Is she okay?" He eyed the companionway.

"She's fine. I tended to her, um, cut."

"Yeah, mate. Sure."

Jeff took a quick inventory of the seven trackers they'd retrieved. Better than he'd hoped. He and Pax discussed what info they might find when they got back to Miami. Which of course made him think of Sharona, and of how she'd looked just a few moments ago, her dark hair splayed across the bunk, her sexy-adorable smile after she'd bit his neck.

Love bite, she'd said…while wearing his T-shirt. Sweet hell, she was one of a kind. In one day, she'd crawled inside his soul and lit a fire.

"Jeff?"

He blinked and looked at Pax. "Yeah?"

"I was asking if I should I pack them with the rest of the gear, or if you want to hold onto them?"

"Leave 'em here," he said, fingering one of the hot-pink transmitters. With all that had happened today, Jeff was grateful Pax and the crew helped him carry on with the research. And with a woman like Sharona now in his life, he felt more and more like a damn lucky guy.

"You got it," Pax said, then left to pack the laptops.

"Good day's work, Dr. Cruz?"

Jeff's heart gave a hard crash against his ribs when he heard her voice. It was amazing how quickly his body learned to react to her. Would it be the same when they were both in Miami? Jeff couldn't help smiling. No…it would be even better. No matter what the challenge, they would figure it out.

"A very good day's work," he said, trying not to smile too much but probably doing a lousy job. "Though not *perfect*."

"Not yet." She returned his smile while tucking the front of his faded National Rugby League T-shirt into her shorts. Glory be—the woman was a bombshell. "Are we heading back now?"

"We should be at Port Jackson in less than two hours."

"So your top-secret research is over." She picked up a transmitter and held it up to the sun. "Extraordinary how this little thing is such a big deal."

"It is," he agreed. "If all goes well, in a year or so, we'll get the patent and be able to sell them to everyone."

"Why not share it sooner? If it's as innovative as you hope, shouldn't we get the word out?"

Jeff couldn't help grinning at her use of the word "we." It took everything in him not to scoop her up in his arms and see about busting that bunk below deck.

"It's exciting, right?" she added. "Don't you want to shout it from the rooftops?"

"I do," he said after a laugh, loving her enthusiasm. "And you're right—it would speed things up if we shared our findings with certain interested parties. I get calls all the time to discuss my projects."

Her eyebrows shot up. "So, Manny was serious this morning about you being...famous?"

"Um yeah," Jeff said. It was kind of refreshing that Sharona didn't know that side of his life. He was usually able to keep a low profile. Whenever he was recognized on the street, people seldom made the connection that he was the same bloke on TV behind the sunglasses and logoed ball cap on the deck of a boat. After all, he was no Crocodile Hunter.

"I have a love-ate thing with the media right now," he added. "It's complicated and I'd rather not deal with complications unless it's *really* important."

"Well, *I'd* love to see you on TV." She lowered her voice and shifted toward him. "Looking all brave and sexy... fighting off sharks with your bare hands."

"Ha! Like *that* row would end well for me." He laughed. "Plus, I've seen enough cameras to last a lifetime. Tell ya what, though, if I do go on the telly again"—he paused to brush his hand over hers — "it'll be just for you."

A smile curved her lips. "I've never been a groupie before."

"And I've never had one. I guess there's a first for everything."

"It's incredible what you're doing, Jeff. Honestly." The warmth in her voice warmed his heart.

"Today was a team effort, including you."

She snorted. Only from Sharona Blaire could that sound be dainty. "Right. I'm the Julia Roberts to your *Ocean's Eleven* crew."

"Crikey, woman. You've got much better legs that Julia Roberts."

Another snort, accompanied by a blush this time. "My biggest contribution today was sending the last Old Faithful to its watery grave."

"It's forgotten," he said. "I know for a fact we wouldn't have done half as much if you weren't aboard." He touched her arm quickly, then drew away. "Do you really think I'm always this efficient?"

"I had a feeling you were…resourceful." Her teeth sank into her full bottom lip. "Well, I need to call my boss and check in, then I've got a few more…um, auditory items I need to check off." She twirled a lock of hair. "With your assistance, I hope?"

Jeff couldn't help it; he reached out and placed a hand to her cheek, not caring who witnessed the act. "Auditory items, eh?" he said, running his thumb over her skin. "I know the ones you mean. One in particular will require my…full attention."

Her beautiful lips parted and she stared up at him. In

about five seconds, Jeff was going to make a huge fool of himself in front of his crew. He almost didn't care. "After you check in at work, don't forget to call Natalie."

"Who?" she asked a little dreamily.

Jeff laughed. "Your best friend who lives in Hershey, Pennsylvania and spends all her time around chocolate, and she's having issues fighting off a past childhood crush, if I recall last night's conversation. It's her birthday, remember? Maybe you should phone her before your boss."

"I'm hoping we'll be too busy with finishing the audit, and I won't have time to do either."

"Sharona." He smiled, pulling his hand away. "We both have jobs to do, and mine doesn't include tearing off your clothes in front of my men." He loved the way her cheeks flushed pink and her dark eyes shined.

"M-maybe I should get Pax to help me with the rest of the audit and I'll meet you back here when we get to Sydney."

"That's probably a wise idea."

She nodded, grabbed the strap of her bag, and headed away. Though the sultry glance she gave him from over her shoulder shot his core temperature off like a rocket.

For the next hour, Jeff caught up on his own work, answering emails and stowing gear. He kept one eye on Sharona and Pax. His assistant kept appearing at his side, clarifying information to relay to Sharona. He looked more and more beat down each time.

"I don't know why she doesn't just ask you herself," Pax said the third time he came over to Jeff. "It's like she's deliberately trying to stay away from you. You must have run her through the ringer, boss."

Jeff couldn't help chuckling as he rubbed his chin. "I'm

afraid I did."

They were just minutes from port and Jeff was fairly impressed with how he'd been able to control himself. But he knew he was on the verge. When he rounded a corner at the back of the helm, he ran face first into the person he'd been trying to not think about every five seconds.

"Oops," Sharona said.

He smiled as he steadied her, keeping his hands on her arms. He'd never been so happy to see anyone in his life. "Hey. We really have to stop meeting like this. Though I wish you'd spilled your drink again so I'd have to take off your—"

"Sorry—didn't see you," she cut in just as Pax appeared from behind.

Jeff dropped his hands and stepped back. "Hey," he said, running a hand through his hair. "How's it going?"

"We're about done," Sharona said, tucking her tablet into the bag hanging off her shoulder.

"She has a lot of questions about Old Faithful," Pax said, looking relieved. "We both know *you're* the man for that job, so I'll let you take over." He patted Jeff on the arm and as he breezed by to exit, he bumped Jeff's shoulder, causing him to step forward into Sharona. He didn't fight the reflex to take her by the arms again, pulling her body close.

"Thank you, Pax," she said, while keeping her eyes on Jeff.

Pax may have replied, but Jeff only heard buzzing behind his ears, because a second later, Sharona's hands slid inside his T-shirt. His body quivered in surprised pleasure.

"Hi," she said.

"Nice to see you. I hope Pax was—" His voice cut off when her fingers hooked under the waistband of his jeans.

"Hmm. If that's a challenge, Ms. Blaire," he said, staring down into her eyes.

"It's a reminder.

Like he needed one of those. Jeff dipped his chin and growled. "I would call you a tease, but I happen to know you're not in any position to make good on your...reminder."

Sharona's hands slid across his bare stomach and around to his back.

"Speaking of positions," he said, walking them until her back hit the wall of the helm. Jeff had a moment of déjà vu, how he'd pinned her to this very wall hours ago. Not to be outdone, he found the bottom of her shirt, tugged free the tucked-in front and slid his hands in, feeling her soft skin as he ran his fingers up her sides, stopping when they brushed lace.

"Jeff," she exhaled in a shaky whisper. "I'm buzzing."

He dipped his chin to her ear. "So am I, baby."

"No, I mean my phone. I've got a call."

It took a moment for the words to compute. "Oh." Quite unwillingly, he slid his hands out from under her shirt. Sharona did the same, then reached inside her bag.

"Damn," she muttered. "Boss."

"I thought you already phoned him."

"Not yet," she said, stepping away from the wall. "I was putting it off. I should answer, though. He's called twice."

"Of course." Jeff took his own step back, giving her room. "We're pulling into port. It's almost over."

"Finally. Though I wouldn't mind ten more minutes downstairs." She bit her lip. "How much time do we have?"

Jeff exhaled a chuckle. "Not enough for me." He bent forward to her ear. "I want you alone," he whispered, gliding a hand around her hip, "on a slow boat to China. Days together, nights…rocking on the waves."

A burst of hot breath was her reply as she fisted the front of his shirt.

"But since I can't have that," he dropped his hand, "I'll let you take care of that call."

"Jeff." She giggled and shoved at his chest. "You'll pay for that." She laughed again, sounding carefree like she had at the bar, then she took a few long strides away, her phone to her ear. "Oh, Jeff, about my boss, remind me to tell you something about him."

"Sure thing." He was still grinning over the pink flush that had stained her cheeks while he walked onto the deck. Packing up had never been such a pleasure. He whistled the chorus to the old folk song "Waltzing Matilda" as he slid his laptop in its case and zipped it up, and after a contented exhale, he stared toward the familiar sight of the Sydney Opera House and the other landmarks. Part of him always felt like coming home, even though he hadn't lived here in years. But family ties never disappeared. He felt more optimistic about the future than he had for a long time. And he knew why.

"Dr. Cruz, would you call today a success?"

He turned to see Leo. The last person in Australia he felt like talking to. But part of Jeff's job was to put on a gracious professional face about marine biology.

"I'd definitely say it was a success."

Leo sat at his side in a bolted-down chair. "I've got my own take, but would you care to elaborate?"

Jeff glanced past the reporter toward the companionway. He'd so much rather be alone with Sharona—on that slow

boat to China—than giving an interview.

"Are we on the record?"

Leo nodded.

Okay, fine. "As you know, we recovered seven trackers, which alone is monumental due to the successful live test of the detachment system, though we won't know the exact information obtained until we plug in at the labs." He answered more of Leo's questions, all the while keeping an eye on the helm.

"Thanks for this," Leo said, sliding a pencil behind an ear. "I appreciate you being so forthcoming, even though you didn't have to be. You could've thrown me overboard, right?"

He paused as if he expected Jeff to disagree.

"I mean, I know it's a hassle having non-crew members aboard but looks like it worked out for everyone. Even the hottie accountant saw her fair share of action."

Jeff couldn't help laughing, then covered his smile with a fist. "Too right."

"Not a bad set up for her," Leo added, rummaging through his satchel. "Flying around the world on the company's dime. I'm sure she gets to pick her own projects since she's engaged to the guy in charge."

Jeff must have heard wrong. "Who's engaged?"

"The hottie. Muh-muh-muh-myyyy Sharona."

Jeff glanced toward the helm them back at Leo, a hard ball in the pit of his stomach. "Why do you think that?"

Leo didn't reply for a moment. "Well, I guess it's okay for me to tell you now. SED hired me, though I really *was* recruited through UM."

"Wait a minute." Jeff held up a hand, forcing himself to

block out the more important information. "The same firm who sent an independent auditor also sent a reporter?"

They both turned when they heard Sharona's laugh and chatter from around the corner, a one-sided conversation—most likely with her boss.

Her *fiancé*.

As he turned back to Leo, Jeff felt ice in his veins. "What makes you think she's engaged to her boss?"

The reporter shrugged. "The guy said so when he hired me a few days ago. He also told me not to say anything because of his job. I guess it's been hush-hush from the beginning. To tell the truth, at first I didn't understand *why* I was here, but when I told him about your transmitters this morning…" He pointed at one on the table. "He's invested thousands in something similar. Seemed kinda shady to me, especially after I talked to him earlier today. Refused to tell him any more about Old Faithful. Dude, those are seriously so cool." He adjusted his backward baseball cap. "Anyway, he said it didn't matter what I did because his fiancée would tell him what he needed to know."

The ice in Jeff's veins started to boil. "I see," he said through a clenched jaw. "Well, I appreciate you not disclosing anything."

Leo shrugged and slid his hands in his back pockets. "My career is just starting; that's not the kind of reporter I want to be. Between you and me, though, that guy at SED is a major prick. Not who I see Sharona with. You were around her today, doing the audit, I hope you didn't share intel that might fall into the wrong hands."

The words stung, especially coming from Leo. Though he wasn't turning out to be such a weasel after all. At least he was loyal. Unlike…

Had the whole thing been an act? Jeff had joked with Sharona earlier about their meeting at the pub being a set up. He hadn't really believed it was true, that a kindhearted, genuine woman like her was capable of coldhearted deception.

Why was she really here? And what had she just said about wanting to tell him something about her boss? A ball of fury rolled in Jeff's chest. Not for the first time in his life, he felt used.

Automatically, his mind flashed to the last time he'd trusted the wrong person with secret, work-relation information, and the disaster that followed. He dumped out the bag carrying the rest of the trackers and spread them across the table. *Why are there only six?* His mind flashed to Sharona examining one a few minutes ago. His stomach dropped in disappointment, but that was quickly replaced by rage.

"Something wrong?" Leo asked.

"I'm missing one," Jeff said, then cursed under his breath.

"Oh, sorry, man. I was curious." Leo placed the missing tag on the table.

Jeff glared at him, wanting to tear him a new one for touching his stuff. But that wasn't what he was really angry about. He blew out a few sharp breaths, but the knot in his stomach wouldn't go away. The fire of doubt was lit and flaming hot.

"Anyway," Leo added, "thanks again for not kicking me off this morning."

"Yeah," Jeff muttered, trying to put on a professional smile. The kid had ended up being his unlikely ally against the most duplicitous of predators.

After Leo wandered off, Jeff stared toward the arching sun that spilled gold across the harbor. He clenched his fists and breathed out his nose, much like he had ten hours ago when he'd first learned that UM was sending a surprise auditor for no bloody good reason.

Now he knew why.

He should've trusted his gut and not let her aboard. No, that wasn't the answer. He should have kept his damn hands to himself and learned from his mistakes. He should've stopped the runaway train before he lost his heart to a woman he couldn't have.

Not only had she disappeared last night and driven him crazy, but then he'd allowed her to get under his skin the very next day. Jeff shook his head, disgusted with himself. He knew better.

"Hey you…"

The voice that had once flooded his body with desire now hit him like nails on a chalkboard. More than anger directed at Sharona, he was pissed at himself for being a big enough chump to fall in love with her in one day.

"Hi," he replied, looking the other way. He'd rather she just leave—he wasn't in the habit of yelling at women and didn't want to start now. Bogie threw him the other end of the rope after securing the *Mad Hatter* to the dock.

"So, I was thinking…" He felt her come up behind him. "Why don't you finish here and we'll meet later so you can help me with that last auditing item I mentioned—"

"You can go now," Jeff said, finally looking at her.

Her mouth fell open and she stared at him. "I…was about to."

Love Bites

There was confusion in her voice and hurt in her brown eyes, but Jeff looked away before it could affect him, winding the rope around his elbow and shoulder.

"Is something wrong?"

He took a breath before looking at her again, noticing the small wheelie suitcase in one hand and her other bag strapped over her shoulder. She had information about Old Faithful and was probably about to sell it to the highest bidder. And there wasn't a damn thing he could do about it.

"You need to leave," he muttered, trying to stay calm while angry heat burned in his chest. "We're at the dock and there's no reason for you to stay. This was a mistake—*my* mistake."

"What mistake? Jeff?"

"I'm so done with these games." He stared at her seemingly innocent face, determined to not back down. "Everything's been a game with you from the very beginning." He raked a hand through his hair. "Why don't you just admit it? Report whatever you want to your *boss*. I can't stop you."

"Jeff—"

He held up a hand.

Fool me once, shame on you. Fool me twice…

"How can I make it any clearer that I'm not interested?" he said, forcing coolness and indifference into his voice. "You admitted how you used me last night to get out of your comfort zone or whatever, but I don't make it a habit of screwing unavailable women, so…" He nodded toward the dock.

She pressed her lips together and glared at him. "You're an *ass*."

He couldn't help scoffing a dark laugh, but the anger was forced. His feelings for her wouldn't go away just like that. The woman he'd thought she was—he still wanted her. But that person was a fantasy he'd dreamed up…the perfect woman who made him happy and shared his passion and kissed him like they were sharks in deep water.

He had no idea who the real Sharona Blaire was. And he couldn't allow himself to care.

"Yep, sweetheart, I sure am," he stated, then walked away.

He tried to block it out completely, but Jeff couldn't help hearing her speak to Manny, her wordless voice floating across the air, coiling around his inner ear…inside is brain.

What the hell was she going on about for so long?

Finally, he heard her little suitcase on wheels roll up the dock away from the ship.

In between muttered curses, Jeff kept himself busy gathering the rest of his gear and seeing off the remaining members of the team. Despite the mess with Sharona, it had been an extremely productive day—he needed to focus on the positive. There was so much data about to be revealed, thanks to the trackers. He hated to admit that earlier he'd even been excited to share his findings with Sharona.

"That's the last of it?" Pax asked when they were about ready to deboard.

"Yep. Good work today."

"Always a pleasure, boss. You heading back to the hotel or straight to the airport with the rest of us?"

"Neither," Jeff said. "I think I'll spend a few days with the rellies." Normally, Jeff *would* catch the first flight out, but he wanted to see his family. He only made it to Oz a few

times a year. His mum would never forgive him if he didn't drop in for a day or two. Plus, his family would be a welcome distraction from the disappointment weighing on his heart.

"Good deal," Pax said. "I'll catch you at the lab next week."

"See you then, mate." Jeff waved him off with a big smile, but dropped it the second his back was turned. He stared off toward the setting sun, trying not to feel anything.

"You hurt that little girl's feelings."

Manny leaned against the front of the helm, his captain's cap cocked to the side.

"She has no feelings," Jeff muttered under his breath. Then he *did* feel like an ass. He sighed. "She's not who she said she was. She wasn't here to do an audit but to find out about Old Faithful."

Manny folded his arms. "What makes you think that?"

"Leo. Did you know *he* was sent by SED, too, not just the uni?" He shook his head and stared down at the deck. "The whole thing was a setup from the beginning. Even last night."

"Last night?"

Why not 'fess up everything?

"Yeah." Jeff rubbed his chin, in desperate need of a shave. "She and I met at the hotel pub."

"I know." Manny was smiling. "She told me."

"Why would she…?"

"I don't think she meant to. Before she left, she pulled me aside again. She was really upset."

Jeff raked both hands through his hair. "So am I."

"Yeah well it sounds a little worse for her, mate. You're not on the verge of being sacked."

"Why would she be sacked? She's engaged to her boss. They planned this whole pleasure cruise." He kneaded the back of his neck, ready to walk away and forget everything, but Manny moved to block his path.

"She's not engaged to her boss."

"Yes, she is. She—"

"They were but she broke it off—six months ago, is what she told me."

Jeff dropped his arms and stared at him.

"She kept working with him because she believed in what she's doing, but she's not involved with him." He shrugged. "From the little she told me, the guy sounds like a Grade-A wanker."

Jeff closed his eyes as his stomach dropped in a gut-wrenching free fall.

"Buddy," Manny said. "You *are* an ass, just like she said."

"Yeah." Why had he trusted the word of some guy off the street but not Sharona—not even ask her about it? He knew why, and it made him despise himself that his past had blinded him so badly.

"Son of a bitch," he muttered, staring toward where he'd last seen her, when she'd looked so hurt and called him an ass. He was, because of how he'd treated her. Picturing her wounded expression made his heart collapse in on itself.

"Do you know where she went?"

"No. But I got the impression she was going home."

"I have to get to her first," Jeff said, turning on his heels and breaking into a run.

Manny chuckled. "Dangerous to stop a moving airplane, mate!"

Jeff spotted Leo down on the dock taking to one of the

crew. "Hey!" he called, jumping over the railing and onto the dock.

"Hey," Leo said. "I was waiting to talk to you. Sorry, man, I totally shot my mouth off with some bad information about Sharona—or it was *outdated* info—"

"I know about that," Jeff cut in. "Look, do you have any local connections with the media?"

Leo scratched his head. "I know one guy, yeah."

Jeff took in a breath. This just might work. "You might want to call him. I think he'll be interested in what's about to happen."

Chapter Ten

"Nat, you must be at work, or maybe it's the middle of the night there, I don't know." Sharona sighed into her cell. "Call me when you can, please? I really need to talk and... oh..." She tried to swallow the lump in her throat. "Happy birthday." She sniffed. "Sorry if I'm a day late. I love you. Call me."

She lowered her phone, then slumped in the backseat of the cab, staring out at the lights of downtown Sydney. It was like she'd fallen down a rabbit hole and had been living another life. In twenty-four hours so much had happened.

She didn't regret any of it until now.

What the freak had gotten into Jeff? She hadn't been playing games. Okay, last night was sort of a game, but weren't they both in on it? And today could not have been more real. How she felt about him...

What hurt worse now was knowing she'd never see him again. She thought they'd had something.

And it was gone. Like it never happened. Like the whole day had been swallowed by Matilda in the blink of an eye.

It had taken way too long to grab a cab at the harbor. So many tourists and then bumper-to-bumper traffic. She was totally dragging by the time she made it to the hotel. The lobby was packed with people, so she skirted along the outside toward the elevator bay.

"Why is it so crowded?" she asked as she passed the concierge desk.

"There's a wedding party," he said in an accent so thick she could barely understand. "They've most of the sleeping rooms at the hotel and they're taking over the rooftop bar tonight. It's open to select guests—my discretion. They even hired a band. Should be a rager." He tilted his head. "Looks like you could use one, luv."

She blew out a tired breath. "Being around a group of people is the last thing I need."

"Know what I always say…when a party is the last thing you want, that's when you need it the most. It's casual dress and an open bar. Gorgeous night under the stars."

Sharona sighed again. "When does it start?"

• • •

After a long shower that was meant to clear her head, she sat on her bed and pulled out the tablet she'd been carrying around all day. As a professional, she shouldn't write up her report on today's audit until she'd cooled off. In her current frame of mind, Jeff Cruz and his precious research team would not get the most glowing endorsement. But the longer she stewed, the more she knew she needed to get it out before she got really pissed.

So she logged onto her computer.

Two hours later, after blow-drying her hair and running a hot iron over her last clean top, Sharona pulled on a pair of dark-wash jeans and headed to the top floor of the hotel. As she was about to enter the crowded rooftop bar, a wave of nostalgia hit, and she froze.

I might not be ready for this.

But one setback—as fresh as it was—should not keep her from being around people. And maybe, like the concierge suggested, disappearing into a sea of strangers was the best thing for her tonight.

She managed to find an empty stool at the far end of the bar.

"Long day, yeah?" the bartender asked over the noise of celebrating, music and clinks of glasses. She had long red hair and a commiserative, bartendery smile.

Sharona exhaled. "You could say that."

"What'll it be?"

She leaned her elbows on the bar. "A new brain and a time machine. Maybe some man repellant?"

The bartender laughed. "How about a triple cocktail? Courtesy of the happy couple."

"Sounds great, thanks," Sharona said, pulling back a grateful smile, though the effort gave her a headache.

"So, guy problems?"

Sharona pushed around a bowl of beer nuts. "Yeah."

"I'm Sigrid," she said, placing a coaster on the bar.

"Nice to meet you."

"Right. So, tell me. What'd he do? Sleep around? Lie? Believe me, I've heard it all."

"Nothing like that. Though he didn't really tell me, he just kind of…flipped out. And when I tried to ask…"

"Wouldn't let you get a word in edgewise?" Sigrid shook her head. "Yeah, men get so proud and cocky when we show the slightest hint of jealousy, but if *we* don't trust them, they fly off the handle."

"They do, don't they?" She gritted her teeth. "They can be such…pigs."

"*Sharks*," Sigrid tagged on, making Sharona's stomach twist like she was aboard the *Mad Hatter* in rough water.

As much as she was trying to forget about it or at least stay angry, a sad rawness squeezed her heart when she thought about Jeff. She'd tried to hold onto the anger as she'd written her report, but the more she wrote, the more she remembered what had really happened, the purpose of today's expedition. She'd learned that Jeff Cruz was a good man, a brilliant scientist, and a tremendous humanitarian, willing to do the right thing by his beloved great white sharks—even if that meant slowing down his research.

After she'd emailed her report to Garry, she'd sat on the hotel bed and tried to ignore the fresh wave of disappointment. The anger was gone, leaving sadness and confusion in its place.

What had he meant about screwing unavailable women? She'd been completely available for six months…ever since she'd broken off her engagement to…

"*Garry*," she growled aloud.

"That his name?" Sigrid asked. "What a bloody prick."

"No. *That's* the name of the lying sack of crap who's been telling lies about our relationship." She shook her head. "So typical of him to do something like this. Oh, I am *so* quitting that job. And then I'm siccing the FCC on his ass, not to mention slapping him with sexual harassment." She dropped her arms on the bar, feeling a combination of anger and helplessness.

"The thing about Jeff," she added a moment later.

"That's the other one?" Sigrid asked.

She nodded. "One minute we were about to break a bunk and... Anyway, the next minute he was yelling at me like...like he didn't trust me. But I don't know why he'd feel that way."

"It's an insecurity thing," Sigrid said, sagely, placing a drink before her.

"Maybe." But Jeff had never once seemed insecure to her. In fact, he was the most put-together and driven guy she'd ever met. That was one of the things that was so dang appealing. "Anyway, thanks for listening." She touched the glass but didn't drink. "I'm Sharona, by the way."

Sigrid slapped her hand on the bar. "No shit, really?"

Sharona rolled her eyes. "I know, just like the song."

"Not what I mean." Sigrid grabbed a folded-up slip of paper off the back of the bar. "A bloke was in here earlier. Left this." She passed Sharona the note.

Sharona, you'll never know how sorry I am, but I sincerely hope you'll give me the chance to explain. It was a big misunderstanding—my fault! And I'm so sorry. ~J

She folded the paper, her mind in a whirl. "Jeff was here?" She glanced around the rooftop bar, dimly lit by twinkle lights and the full moon above.

"Never got his name," Sigrid said. "As you can see, it's pretty dark up here. Is he a tall guy, brown hair, amazingly good-looking?"

Sharona's throat tightened unexpectedly as tears welled behind her eyes. "That's him. Do you know where he went?"

"After he made all the barkeeps and waiters memorize your name and told them about the note here, he dropped a big tip and left. Seemed desperate to find you. Can you call him?"

"I don't...know..."

She scanned the bar, feeling wretchedly out of place among the happy wedding guests. Just over Sigrid's head were three flat-screen TVs, one showing a soccer game, one playing a montage of photos—probably of the newlyweds—and the third screen had the local news.

Sharona sighed and leaned on an elbow, but when a new news story flashed across the screen, she sat up straight. "Turn it up!" she called to Sigrid, pointing at the third screen.

The bartender grabbed a remote, increasing the volume.

Sharona still couldn't hear it, but she could see Jeff on-screen perfectly. He wore a white polo shirt with a red-and-blue logo over the pocket. The visor he'd been wearing earlier today had sported the same logo.

She recognized the helm of the *Mad Hatter.* The sun was setting behind him, so this must've been shot a few hours ago—after they'd docked. Right after she'd left. Manny stood behind him, and was that...Leo with a mic in his hand? Jeff held something...something about the size of a magic marker...something hot pink.

"I can't hear him," Sharona said, about to scale the bar so she should stick her ear to the speaker. "Can you hear what Jeff's saying?"

Sigrid stared at her, slack-jawed. "*That's* him? You're talking about Jeff Cruz? Jeff Cruz was in my bar and I didn't recognize him? Son of a—"

"What's he saying?" Sharona cut in, and then looked at Sigrid. "How do *you* know him?"

"Girl, that's Great White Cruz. He used to be on the local news all the time—hometown bloke makes good with his dream team of shark men. He has a huge following around here, but about a year ago he went underground." She turned back to the screen with new interest. "He's…he's saying that it's time to reveal new technology." She paused to listen. "He says he was afraid he'd lose what's most important to him but someone close to him said it was time to share. Something about trust and taking a leap of faith. Wait…hold on." Sigrid rose up on her toes as Sharona's gaze flashed back and forth from her to the screen.

"What's he saying now?"

"Something about…eh?"

Sharona's eyes grew large. "What?" she begged.

"That George Clooney movie, *Ocean's Eleven*."

Sharona stared at the screen as Jeff smiled and looked directly into the camera lens, speaking words she couldn't hear.

"He says he's looking for a missing member of his crew, his—"

"Julia Roberts," they said together.

Sigrid turned to her. "He's talking about you?"

Without a thought, Sharona kicked off her shoes and climbed onto the slippery, polished bar, grabbing the screen with both hands. If she couldn't get to the real Jeff Cruz, she sure as hell was going to hear every damn word TV Jeff was saying.

"Come down, sweetie," said another bartender. "Sig, no more whiskey for this one."

"Shut up," Sharona hissed, pressing her ear against the speaker. But all she heard was the weather report. She stared at the screen. "Where'd he go?" she demanded, gazing down at Sigrid.

"It's gone to commercial," she replied. "Let's get you another drink."

A group of guys at a table started whistling and catcalling, requesting Sharona give *them* a table dance.

"I'm all about grand gestures in the name of love," Sigrid called up to her over the noise, "but I reckon the manager's gonna ring the cops if you don't come down. Chicks like you will cause a riot."

Sharona bit her lip, suddenly realizing where she was.

"Oh, shit," she whispered, unable to move. She covered her face in her hands, like that would make her disappear.

"Jim, Curly," she heard Sigrid say. "Help her down. Come on, luv. Give us your hand."

"I've got her."

The deep, familiar voice sounded like a dream in her head. Then a warm hand had her around her ankle. She opened her eyes to see Jeff gazing up.

"Baby. What are you doing up there?" he asked, lightness and curiosity in his voice.

All she could do is point at the screen. "You were… there…"

"Come down. I really need to talk to you." He reached up a hand. Sharona was about to take it but then stopped.

"Talk?" She folded her arms. "About what?"

Just then, the band started playing "YMCA" and no one seemed to care about the crazy lady standing on the bar any more.

"Come down," Jeff said, waving his hand.

She shook her head. "You said you need to talk…so talk."

"I can't hear you, babe," he said over the growing volume of the music. "Come on."

But she wasn't budging. Jeff dropped his outstretched arm and she could see him exhale in frustration. He looked clean, shaven, and gorgeous by light of the moon. He wasn't wearing the white polo shirt with the logo, but a blue T-shirt and dark jeans. It was hard to believe he was the same man who'd just been on TV, when all she could see was the guy hovering over her in a tiny bunk — when he'd been all hers.

"Fine!" he finally called, cupping his hands around his mouth. "I'm sorry, okay?"

"About what?"

He didn't go on right away but lowered his hands to his hips. "I was…misinformed about your relationship status." He glanced over his shoulders, probably feeling more than a little conspicuous. After a throat clear, he continued. "I was also misinformed as to why you'd been sent by SED. I'm sorry for those things I said. I was an ass."

She widened her eyes.

"Okay, a *huge* ass."

"You should've asked me about it," she called.

"I know. I know." He nodded up and down. "I have a problem with trust and…with putting my heart on the line and going all in for what I *really want* and…" He paused to shake his head, running a hand through his hair with a sexy, self-deprecating smile. "I reacted before I thought, figured it out too late." He touched her bare foot, then circled his hand around her calf. The gentle contact was in complete opposition to the forcefulness of his voice as he called, "Sharona, I'm sorry. Do you believe me?"

She couldn't help pressing her lips together and smiling. After such a delicious display, the answer was too easy. "Yes," she said, her heart tripping over the single word.

He balked back, looking surprised. "Yeah?"

"Uh-huh."

"Then will you please come here?" He reached up. She took his hand and bent forward so he could take her by the waist and hoist her down. He did so, a bit more roughly than she'd expected after his heroic, chivalrous exhibition.

"You're insane," he muttered, dropping onto a bar stool. He was so adorably embarrassed, it was an actual struggle to not fall in love with him on the spot. "So, you saw the news, I gather?"

She nodded. "But the volume was too low and I couldn't hear... I saw Old Faithful."

"Sit." He pointed at the seat beside him and she sat. "You were right. I needed to talk about our research and some other things. I'm glad I did, and I'm really glad you saw it." He paused and shifted closer to her. "I was afraid you'd go straight to the airport, but I still had to look for you, I had to *try*." He sighed. "The front desk wouldn't tell me if you had a reservation, but I hoped you were here. Never imagined I'd find you on top of a bar."

"Yeah, well." She bit her lip. "I was trying, too."

He took her hand and pulled her so her knees were

between his. "This can work," he said, staring into her eyes. "I know it can."

"After your little broadcast," she gestured at the TV, "you know you're going to be on the Discovery Channel again—and you *should* be. You've got such an important job." She pulled back her hand. "What if being with me— because of *my* job…what if that messes it up and—"

"See." Jeff cut her off. "*This* is what I like about you. You think of others first. You almost got swallowed by a shark, yet your first words to me were about losing the bloody tracker." He took her hand again, sandwiching it between his so she couldn't pull away. "You were thinking of me, and I love you for that."

Sharona felt her heart grow light, wanting so much to believe his words. Maybe she needed to take her own leap of faith. And it wasn't just physical. She was drawn to Jeff for so many reasons that she hadn't known existed when they'd first met at that very hotel.

"Sharona Blaire." Scooting closer, Jeff touched her cheek and ran a thumb along her skin, making every cell tingle. "Please forgive me. Don't say my idiotic mistake ruined the greatest love story since Jonah and the whale."

"Jeff…" She felt tears behind her eyes. "Of course I forgive—"

The sensation of his lips on hers was just as stunning as the first time. She felt the buzz down to her toes. With their mouth attached, he put his hands on the sides of her neck and she wound her arms around him, feeling safe and protected, like she did each time they were together.

His breath was sweet and welcoming against her skin when he whispered her name. From over his shoulder, she caught Sigrid's eye. She gave her a tiny nod, then went back to her other customers.

Remembering something, Sharona pulled back. "Jonah and the whale?" she whispered, staring into his eyes.

Jeff laughed. "Marine biology humor."

"That's so hot." She grinned. As the band played another hit from the seventies, Jeff's hands found their way inside her shirt. Before they explored too far, a group of wedding guests bellied up to the bar.

"I think they want our spot," Jeff said, his mouth against her neck.

"They can have it," she whispered. "Hey, are you up for one more game?"

"Sharona…" he warned.

"Not even role-playing?"

Jeff pulled back and eyed her. "Oh, baby."

She ran a hand up his thigh. "We should pretend like we just met."

"Like we're total strangers and I pick you up at a bar?"

"Or *I* pick *you* up."

Jeff's hands glided along the skin of her back, one finger skimming across where her bra strap should have been. He pulled away to look her in the eyes. "You're not wearing a…" Slowly, she shook her head and he cocked one of his crooked Han Solo grins. "Sweet mother of…"

"Back to our game," she prompted.

"Right." Jeff removed his hands from her back. "So we just met. What comes first? Your call."

"First…" She placed her hands on his chest, then slid them around his neck. "I kiss you." She pressed her lips to his, hard, until her head went beautifully fuzzy.

"I like that," Jeff whispered, hovering over her mouth. "Then I kiss you and do this." New sparks shot behind her closed eyes as Jeff's hands cupped her butt and deftly pulled her onto his lap, her legs straddling him. "What's next?"

"Next"—she managed to breathe out—"I notice your sexy accent and ask if you're from these parts."

He repositioned her on his lap, then kissed her nose. "And I say I live in Miami but grew up an hour from here. Then I ask if you'd like to come home with me tomorrow."

Sharona pulled back. "Meet your family?"

"Too fast for having met five minutes ago?" He rubbed his nose against her cheek. "They'll absolutely love you, Sharona. Do you have to fly home tomorrow?"

"I'm supposed to, but I already turned in my report and…" She grinned, feeling butterflies in her stomach and a coiling tension in her core. "I'm allowed a little vacation. And thank you for the invitation. It means so much to me." She kissed him slowly, forgetting how to think, how to breathe.

"I'm anxious to see what happens next," Jeff said, moving his warm hands to her hips and sliding her off his lap she could stand. "I've only been picked up at a pub once before."

Sharona smiled, while trying to stay upright. "Well, since you're also visiting, the polite thing would be for you to invite me to your room…show me your shark bite." She tugged at the front of his shirt, then slid in a hand, touching the slick band of scars on his stomach, feeling his muscles contract. "I have no words, Jeff Cruz"—she paused and touched her forehead to his—"to explain how sexy you are. But I can't wait to show you."

"Ditto," he said with a grin, cupping a hand over her hip

then gliding down. "Just to warn you, I don't give my love bites on the neck."

Hot damn. With her eyes locked on his, she fisted the front of his shirt, pressed her mouth against his and stepped back, forcing him to stand. Lips still connected, she walked him backward through the crowd. Not until they were in the elevator bay did she break the kiss.

"Which floor?" she asked, fighting to catch her breath.

"Floor?" he panted, moving to her neck.

"Which floor is your room?"

He pulled back. "I don't have a room. I planned on going straight to my family tonight. Then something much more important"—he cocked an eyebrow—"came up."

"Oh. Well then, I suppose I'll be inviting you to my room. It's only polite." She stepped out of his arms and pressed the call button. "Wait right here?" she asked. "I'll be back to get you."

Jeff narrowed his eyes. "No bloody way in hell, gorgeous," he whispered, drawing out the words. "Don't think I'm letting you out of my sight this time. Or ever."

Sharona bit her lip and thought about her cluttered hotel room, the unmade bed, her notes and computer and unpacked clothes. Then she looked at Jeff.

As the doors slid open, she stepped into the empty elevator, reached out a hand, and pulled him inside.

"Going down…"

* * *

Acknowledgments

Thank you to the usual suspects…

My Entangled Dream Team: Stacy, Alycia, Heather and Debbie. Writerly friends and non-writerly friends: Sue, Ginger, Nancy, Lisa, Cindi and Rachel. Sara, for lending me both SED Independent Auditors of Miami-Dade County and vile Garry. My family for being cool and excited and supportive. Readers, bloggers, reviewers and all my amazzzzzing social media peeps. Each of you makes me a better writer! Last but not least, The Discovery Channel's "Shark Week," *Jaws* (in all its reincarnated, franchise glory), the supersexy "Shark Men" of National Geographic (including the late Paul Walker…the original inspiration for Jeff Cruz) and all the other killer fish stories that continue to fuel my obsession, love, terror, nightmares and captivation.

About the Author

Ophelia London was born and raised among the redwood trees in beautiful northern California. Once she was fully educated, she decided to settle in Florida, but her car broke down in Texas and she's lived in Dallas ever since. A cupcake and treadmill aficionado (obviously those things are connected), she spends her time watching art-house movies and impossibly trashy TV, while living vicariously through the characters in the books she writes. Ophelia is the author of ABBY ROAD; the Perfect Kisses series including: PLAYING AT LOVE, SPEAKING OF LOVE, and FALLING FOR HER SOLDIER, and the new adult DEFINITELY, MAYBE IN LOVE. Visit her at http:// ophelialondon.com. But don't call when *The Vampire Diaries* is on.

.

Made in the USA
Las Vegas, NV
10 May 2022

48709260R00085